"Unbroken is a journey of the self in all its forms, its methods delicate and vicious, its story sexy and emotional. Brooklyn Ray offers readers another beautiful story that tastes like catharsis; once again we fall in love with a damaged hero, and once again Brooklyn makes us stare through the darkness and see light."

—L.A Ashton author of *Echoes*

"Sexy, dark, and bloody. An exploration of healing and overcoming trauma through raw physical intimacy, told in Brooklyn Ray's beautiful, atmospheric prose and handled with sensitivity and care. A story about demons, both literal and figurative, set in the stormy town of Port Lewis, home to witches, necromancers, ghosts, and magic."

—Piper Vaughn author of *Off the Ice*

"With Unbroken, Brooklyn Ray once more crafts a paranormal romance that is as compelling as it is poignant, with themes of acceptance and recovery from abuse. Michael finds healing in, quite literally, accepting a demon. Victor is equal parts brutal and tender, and is exactly the friend and lover Michael needs. Ray's writing shines in this installment of the Port Lewis Witches."

—Anna Zabo author of *Syncopation*

"The sex scenes [in Darkling] were gorgeous; hot, magical whirlwinds of intensity that were exactly right for the characters and the story, and were also deeply romantic. I loved these aspects of the story, and would name the sex in this book some of the best sex scenes I've read in a romance involving a trans main character."

—Xan West Author of *Show Yourself to Me*

"Queer witchy magic guaranteed to make your toes curl."

—Michelle Osgood author of *The Better to Kiss You With*

"Brooklyn Ray's Unbroken is a sexy and addictive blend of magic and romance that truly shines with its deep character connections and masterful exploration of love, trauma, and healing."

—Alex Harrow, author of *Empire of Light*

# Unbroken

A Port Lewis Witches Story

*Brooklyn Ray*

A NineStar Press Publication

Published by NineStar Press
P.O. Box 91792,
Albuquerque, New Mexico, 87199 USA.
www.ninestarpress.com

# Unbroken

Copyright © 2019 by Brooklyn Ray
Cover Art by Natasha Snow Copyright © 2019

This is a work of fiction. Names, characters, places, and incidents are either the product of the author's imagination or are used fictitiously. Any resemblance to actual persons living or dead, business establishments, events, or locales is entirely coincidental.

All rights reserved. No part of this publication may be reproduced in any material form, whether by printing, photocopying, scanning or otherwise without the written permission of the publisher. To request permission and all other inquiries, contact NineStar Press at the physical or web addresses above or at Contact@ninestarpress.com.

Printed in the USA
First Edition
April, 2019

Print ISBN: 978-1-950412-57-0

Also available in eBook, ISBN: 978-1-950412-42-6

Warning: This book contains sexually explicit content, which may only be suitable for mature readers, depictions of blood play, references to date rape within an abusive relationship, and self-harm.

For those of us who find love in haunted places

# Author's Note

There are scenes and themes in *Unbroken* that might be triggering to some readers. Content warnings are listed below:

Depictions of anxiety, blood play in sexual and non-sexual situations, off-page reference to past sexual abuse within an abusive relationship, self-harm

If you are a survivor of sexual assault or struggle with symptoms brought on by sexual trauma call 800-656-HOPE (4673) or 833-SAFE (7233)-833 to connect with confidential support

# Part One: Haunted Places

MICHAEL GATES CURLED his hand over the old fence surrounding his new home. Splinters nipped at his palm. Bitter wind snapped restlessly at his cheeks. He wasn't used to cold like this, the kind that stuck to his skin and seeped through his clothes. This was coastal cold. Northern Cold. Port Lewis cold.

"I bet you're missin' Arizona right about now, huh?" Janice tossed a grin over her shoulder as she wobbled inside, carrying one end of a mustard yellow couch. She was a broad girl, tall like their father, with candy-apple red hair that came from a box. "Mom probably hasn't converted your room into a yoga studio yet. There's still time!"

Michael snorted. Denying the truth would only lead to more teasing, and he wasn't in the mood to bicker with his sister. Not after a long-ass drive. Not when he still wasn't sure about any of this—college, this town, this *house*.

It was almost charming, he thought. Windows jutted from sharp-edged sills and the attic skewered the sky like a steeple, stretched tall over the porch above a round window on the second floor. The paint had been yellow once, but the sun turned the walls white and the shingles gray. Vines crawled over the empty garden boxes attached to the porch, a burst of green in a colorless place. It was Victorian and strange, and as Michael looked from the creaky steps to the unkempt lawn, he remembered the word their landlord had used during an awkward Skype interview two weeks ago.

*History*, she'd said, like it was a curse.

"Hey, asshole." Janice stood in the doorway with her hands perched on her hips, cheeks flushed and chest heaving. "Movers are heading out. You gonna help me drag these mattresses upstairs before Corey gets here or not?"

There wasn't anything wrong with the house. The windows weren't broken, the kitchen was stocked with upgraded appliances, and the fire alarms had recently been replaced. But wrongness still lingered, somehow.

His fingers slipped off the fence and dove into his coat pocket, thumbing the corner of a cigarette pack. "I didn't even get a chance to smoke."

"Too bad. Those'll kill you anyway, c'mon."

Michael rolled his eyes but reluctantly walked inside. The word kept repeating, whispered like a secret—*history history history*—and he couldn't stop wondering about what a place had to go through to earn it. The floorboards flexed and whined under his boots. Above him, cobwebs dripped from a metal chandelier, and light beamed through the window onto a steep, carpeted staircase. He might've imagined it, must have imagined it, but he swore the air shifted, as if the house had sensed his aching lungs and insisted he take a breath.

"This place is weird," Michael blurted because he had no other way to explain it. "Creepy weird, like I bet someone was murdered here *weird*."

"You're being dramatic," Janice said. She tilted a mattress off the wall and pushed it toward the staircase. Her jaw clenched as they ambled up the stairs, freckled cheeks hollowed and shoulders rounded. They shared many things, like most siblings did. Dark eyes and wide mouths, long fingers and small chins. But where Janice's fine lines and prominent bones made her look strong, Michael's only made him look delicate. He was littered with scars because of it, badges to prove he wasn't breakable.

After three trips up and down the stairs, they flopped the final mattress on the ground in the second-to-last bedroom, and Janice heaved a relieved sigh.

"Michael, c'mon." She nudged him with her elbow, pulling his attention from the boxes scattered on the floor. "This place is just *old*, you know? Look, you've got a balcony"—she pointed to the French doors, then set her hands on his shoulders and steered him toward the hall—"and your own bathroom, and I mean, this is a fresh start for us. Port Lewis is small, but we start classes next week, and there's a movie theater downtown and some really good breweries..."

Michael's lips quirked into a half-smile. "The Pacific Northwest *is* known for its beer."

"Exactly!" Janice gave his shoulders a reassuring squeeze. "Speaking of libations, how about you start unpacking and I'll run out for Thai and a case of IPA, sound good?"

"Fine, sure, whatever," he said, biting back a laugh. "Green curry for me. You should probably text Corey and ask if he wants anything."

Janice swatted the bedroom door on her way out. Her keys jingled, sneakers thudded the stairs, and before Michael could shout—*don't forget the chili paste*—the door slammed and she was gone.

Silence snaked through the house, disrupted by wind pressing on the windows, and the unmistakable inkling that he was being watched. Michael pushed his fingers through his hair, short auburn locks smoothed by product he'd found in his sister's makeup bag, and heaved a sigh.

Janice was right, he told himself. The house was old. It creaked and howled and carried secrets from past owners. But it was just a house, and Michael had seen too many horror movies to let a little unease get the best of him. He rummaged through two boxes until he found a portable speaker.

"There we go," he said, pulse quickening when his own voice echoed through the empty house. He set his phone on the dock and turned on a Pop Punk playlist. Music boomed through his new room, loud and fast, a sore reminder of the home down south and all the memories left behind there. His mother had allowed him to take a gap year after high school, where he spent twelve months abroad, bouncing from Ireland to London, Amsterdam to Italy, but when another year went by and Michael skipped registration at the junior college he'd promised to attend, his family's patience thinned.

*There's no time left to squander,* his mother had said. *Go with your sister, take botany for all I care, but do something.*

So, he'd followed Janice to Port Lewis, a town built on rumors, whispers about magic and witches, and ended up here, sliding the mattress into a black bed frame, listening to songs he'd fallen in love with during senior year, and watching a shadow cross the floor in the reflection on his balcony window.

Michael froze, mouth set and shoulders pulled tight. He held the edge of the mattress, gaze pinned to the reflection in the window, afraid the image would disappear if he moved, and more afraid to turn around. Because there, looking back at him, was a pair of eyes and a curious smile attached to a distorted shape standing in the doorway. His throat cinched and his mouth dried, and all the bravery, all the fight, all the resolve, fell out from under him. He blinked once, twice, a third time, and then it was gone.

*Impossible.* He turned on his heels, expecting an *ah-hah!* An *I got you!* A moment when he'd catch something—someone—hiding in the hallway. But the doorway was empty, and when he peeked into the hall, it was empty too.

"Janice?" He pushed open each bedroom door and looked inside. Nothing. He did the same with the two bathrooms, the linen closet, the cabinets. Nothing. "Corey?"

A sound he faintly recognized came from behind him, far enough away to seem distant, close enough to make his breath quake. Metal on metal. The drag and click of a lock being unfastened.

It was right then he noticed the stagnant air, the heavy quiet. His music was no longer playing.

Michael felt it like he thought all people usually did—a wrongness that settled deep inside him—coupled with the urge to leave, the need to run. But he didn't. He turned slowly this time, reining in his runaway heart, and trailed his gaze up the narrow steps at the end of the hall to the attic door, unlocked, and ajar.

One moment the shadow was there, and a second later it simply wasn't.

"Who are you?" Michael called. He clung to the only bravery he had left. Defiance. The reckless confidence responsible for many of his scars.

The attic door swung open on rusty hinges.

Adrenaline cautioned, but curiosity encouraged, and Michael found each step easier to take as he climbed the stairs. The banister was smooth under his palm, the air alight with danger and magic and something unknown.

Something dark, he thought. Something tarnished.

*Don't*, his heart said. *Run. Go. Now. Now. Now.*

Michael swallowed hard and stepped into the room. Sunlight illuminated moth-eaten curtains in front of the window. A bed was pushed against the wall, sheets tucked, white comforter smoothed. There was a lamp on a black nightstand, unlit candles on a six-drawered dresser, and a bookshelf against the far wall. He crossed the room, trailing his fingers along the edge of the bed, the windowsill, then the shelves, tracing letters on thick leather spines. *Magic & Purpose. Ceremonial Preparation. Incantations.* He plucked a paperback from the middle shelf—*Demonology*—and opened it. The pages were sallow, stained in some places and ripped in others. Sprawling notes in black ink filled the margins. He turned the book over in his hands and found a name written on the inside of the back cover.

"Victor Lewellyn," Michael whispered.

The floorboards whined. Breath hit the back of his neck. A low, smooth voice said, "Michael Gates."

Dread filled the pit of his stomach. He snapped the book shut by the spine, attempted to summon any semblance of the bravery he'd found before, and came away with none. His breath fluttered from him in trembling gusts, and when a warm palm cradled his elbow, a sob caught in his throat.

"Don't be scared," the stranger purred. His hand slid along the underside of Michael's forearm and curled over his wrist. "You say my name like a prayer."

Michael shut his mouth with an audible click and watched Victor Llewellyn's fingers, tipped with black claws, slide over his knuckles and grasp the book. Reality tilted, shifting from a nightmare into something worse. History suddenly seemed like a hollow explanation for what this house had seen.

Victor's lips grazed his pulse, breath steady, touch confident. His voice was strained between his teeth, deep and inhuman and obscurely intimate, pressed to Michael's throat like the clasp on a collar. "Fuck, you smell like honey."

"What..." Michael's lips parted. He rehearsed what he was about to say, repeating it again and again, but the question never materialized. *What are you?* He wanted to ask, he wanted to know, but his voice malfunctioned with Victor's teeth so close to his skin.

Ghosts were real, he believed in that much. Spirits and poltergeists and an in-between that gave the lost a home. But Victor Lewellyn was not a ghost.

Michael's heart drummed, blood coursing fast through his veins. His knees wobbled, his eyes wide and hungry, desperate for a glance. For a memory. For proof. He inhaled deeply and turned until they were chest to chest.

Victor's mouth formed an easy grin, face sculpted by shadows where the light didn't touch and smoothed like polished copper where it did. He looked like a painting, rich and haunted, a canvas that turned beauty into a monstrous thing.

Humans did not have cheekbones as carved as his. They did not have eyes like lit candles, or black horns curling from their temples. They did not have claws that came to rest on the hinge of Michael's jaw, or breath tinged with ash and blood. Humans were familiar. They were simple and safe. Victor was not.

"What are you?" Michael asked, breathless.

Victor tilted his head. A strand of dark hair fell over his brow. His smile softened as he slid the book back where it belonged, tipping Michael's chin toward him with one hand, and effortlessly caging him against the shelf with the other. They stayed like that, watching each other, until the sound of the front door opening broke the silence, and Janice's voice rang through the house.

"Look who I found in the driveway," she hollered. Keys jingled, plastic bags rustled.

Michael glanced at the door, and when he looked back, Victor was gone.

# Part Two: A Soul to Sell

MICHAEL WASN'T A stranger to the idea that impossible things could present themselves in believable ways. He'd heard voices in empty places before, watched shadows jitter across walls, placed his fingertips on a planchette and asked a Ouija board for answers.

But the voices could've been imagined. The shadows could've been a trick of the light. Someone could've pushed the planchette. All those instances could be explained away—*understood*. But Victor Lewellyn did not come with an easy explanation.

He gripped the edge of the vanity and his reflection looked back at him, cheeks hot, skin still warm where Victor's hand had rested beneath his chin. He glanced at each side of his jaw, looking for blood or bruises or something, anything. But Michael's frantic heartbeat was the only thing left. That and regret—not touching the smoothed collar on Victor's shirt or pressing his fingers to those jagged horns. *Touch makes things real,* he thought. Real and visceral and true.

"Michael?" Janice called.

"Yeah, I'm..." He cleared his throat, eyes squeezed shut, bottom lip pinched hard between his teeth. *I'm what?* He glanced at his reflection again, waiting for Victor to appear behind him, for black claws to find his wrist, and sharp teeth to scrape his throat. But he was alone. *I'm losing my mind.* "I'll be right there!"

The hallway seemed longer, narrower, as if the walls leaned close to look at him. He glanced over his shoulder at the attic. The door was closed again, and he assumed Victor and his secrets were locked behind it. The urge still trembled in him. *Go see.* A terrible, desperate thing. *Go get your answers.*

Michael almost tripped as he hurried down the stairs.

Janice leaned against the crowded coffee table and tipped her beer toward Corey who dug through a white takeout box, seated on the kitchen counter. "Finally," she teased. "This is our roommate, Corey Thompson. Corey, this is my brother, Michael."

Corey offered a small smile. He was traditionally handsome in all the ways Michael wasn't, with boyish features and dimpled cheeks. Blond hair was swept out of his face, purposefully messy, and his jeans were the same, shredded and ripped, manufactured to look destroyed.

"Hey," Michael said. He grabbed a beer and placed it against the edge of the counter, snapping the cap off with a hard swat from the heel of his palm. Corey's expression morphed from interested to surprised. "You're a sophomore at the local college, right?"

"Right. You?" Corey had watery blue eyes, pale enough to be unsettling when they lingered too long.

Michael shrugged off his coat and tossed it over the back of the couch, paying mind to the way Corey watched him, how he looked from one tattoo to the next. They weren't pretty—most were the result of too much liquor—but they were his nonetheless. A skull on his knuckle, a rose on the outside of his palm, anchors on his elbows, sparrows and daggers and snakes on his forearms.

"Not sure yet." He sipped his beer and fingered through the plastic takeout bag until he found the jasmine rice, green curry, and thankfully, two packets of chili paste.

"Michael's interested in architecture," Janice said, parroting the same fabricated answer their mother used at every family gathering.

"Smart move. Lots of security in that field if you find the right job," Corey said.

Michael didn't care about security. He didn't care about college or a hefty retirement or impressing his parents. He hadn't cared about it before, and he didn't care about it now. Especially not when his heart was still racing, and his hands were still shaking, and Victor's voice kept playing behind every thought.

*You say my name like a prayer.*

Janice opened her mouth to speak, probably to excuse Michael's shitty social skills. *It was a long drive,* she'd say. *Don't mind him, he's always quiet.* But Michael cut her off before she could.

"Do you know anyone named Victor?" He flicked his eyes from Janice to Corey. "Victor Lewellyn?"

There it was again, seeping through the walls, thickening the air, that wrongness.

Janice's brow furrowed. Her gaze swept to Corey and she shrugged. "Our landlord's last name is Lewellyn, I think. Why?"

Michael shook his head. He didn't know how to explain what he'd seen, and even if he did, Janice wouldn't believe him. He glanced at Corey and waited but received a dismissive shrug rather than an answer.

"Found an old book in my closet, that's all." He shoveled rice into his mouth, trying to keep Victor's name from stumbling out again. It rested on the tip of his tongue, and like the wrongness and the quiet, Michael found himself drawn to it.

Janice barked a laugh, but despite her best efforts, the silence remained.

Corey pushed noodles around with his chopsticks, eyes settling somewhere else every other second. He was nervous. Intimidated, maybe. Michael tossed his empty bottle in the recycling bin, broke the cap off another beer, and shrugged toward the stairs.

"It's late and I still gotta unpack a bunch of shit. Breakfast in the morning?" The invitation was an olive branch, but a genuine one. "Corey, you know any good places around town?"

"A few," Corey said. His smile stretched into a grin, confirming nervousness rather than intimidation. "What time?"

"Ten." Michael tossed the word over his shoulder.

The stairs creaked again. The walls leaned in close again.

Janice and Corey chattered downstairs. His name was whispered between them, accompanied by *single* and *player* and *lonely*. All true things, no matter how often he denied it.

But his past didn't matter. Not here, in Port Lewis, in this house where history was synonymous with haunted.

Michael pinched the neck of the bottle between two fingers and walked into his bedroom, greeted by his unmade bed and unpacked boxes, his phone still perched on the speaker dock, and Victor, his golden eyes and jagged horns, silhouetted on the balcony.

THERE WAS NOTHING right about this. Michael was aware enough to understand that. However, he lacked an efficient moral compass and usually found himself in unpredictable situations because of it.

This was one hell of a *situation*.

He hadn't taken his eyes off the dark shape lingering on his balcony, not as the door shut, not as he twisted the lock, not even as he crossed the room, stepping between boxes and piles of clothes, and stood with his feet poised at the edge of the carpet. The white lace curtain tied to the top of the French door billowed gently, a whisper dividing Michael from Victor.

"Hello again," Victor said. His eyes caught the light from inside, glinting like a cat's would. He sighed, a far too human sound for someone who had transcended their humanness. "Boneyard, huh? Good choice."

Michael blinked. He replayed what Victor said, trying and failing to understand. His lips parted and a warm gust fogged the air in front of his mouth. Victor appeared before he could speak. One moment he'd stood near the balcony wall, far enough away that the darkness shrouded him, and a second later, his clawed fingers curled effortlessly around the neck of the bottle.

"Are you going to answer my question?" Michael asked. He tipped his head back, leaning away from Victor's smile before it pressed into his skin. Victor's thumb brushed his wrist, a simple, fleeting touch. "What..." Michael closed his eyes. "What the hell are you?"

A laugh, stunted and low, bloomed in Victor's throat. He tugged the cold bottle from Michael's hand and lifted it to his mouth. "I've missed this, you know." He took a sip, then another. "Craft beer. Not, like, *your coworker's friend brewed it in their basement* craft beer, but—" He met Michael's eyes and took another swig. "—the good stuff."

Michael sidestepped into the middle of the balcony. His eyes trailed the horizon where tall trees worked a jagged pattern between the dark navy sky and the black mountain peaks in the distance. He was not naïve enough to believe Victor would be gone when he glanced over his shoulder, and somehow, he hoped for the opposite.

The bottle nudged his hand and Michael took it without question. He tipped it against his mouth, still warm and slick from Victor's lips, and took a sip.

"I'm a few things." Victor spoke like someone who had lived long enough to know the difference between fear and being afraid. One was an essence—a tangible thing that filled a room, and the other was a state of mind. Michael recognized fear, felt it stirring the air around them, but this time he wasn't afraid. "I'm the son of Chastity Drake, Second to Margo Lewellyn, matriarch of the Pacific Northwest Lewellyn clan."

Michael's eyes drifted from the horizon to where Victor stood, bathed in the light from a dim outdoor lamp above the door. Gray moths bounced off the bulb. Victor's copper skin glowed, his face suddenly softer, horns gone where they'd sprouted from his temples seconds ago, fingers long, elegant, and clawless.

"And that makes me a witch," Victor added. He lifted his chin, lashes dark as an oil spill across his cheeks, and swept his gaze from Michael's boots to his nose. He held his arms out. "This is what I was before I died eleven months ago."

*Handsome*, Michael thought. *Normal.* "What..." He didn't want to repeat himself. *What are you, what are you, what are you?* It was a tired question, and he didn't think asking it would get him an answer. "What did you become?"

A confident stride beneath the light and Victor closed the distance between them. Shadows stretched and bent, chasing away the illusion and revealing the wicked thing from before. Horned and regal, etched with bones that pushed too hard against his skin and a smile that curved like a crescent moon.

"Powerful," Victor whispered. He looked down his nose at Michael, head tipped to catch his gaze, and tugged the bottle from his hand. "I had something to sell and a buyer willing to wait, but unfortunately my timing was off, and"—another sip, another smile—"the deal I'd made went through quicker than I thought it would."

*Witch. Sell. Buyer. Powerful.*

Michael pulled a cigarette from the pale blue pack in his coat pocket. He willed his hands to stay steady, but they trembled around the lighter, thumb on the metal wheel, flicking and sparking. "Fuck..." The curse sounded immature, a naïve attempt at feigning confidence. Michael's ears turned pink and his cheeks heated.

"Impatient," Victor said. His hand came to rest on Michael's jaw, claws sharp on his skin. Everything tilted. The balcony. Michael's thoughts. The air in his chest. The night sky. Michael watched, enraptured, as Victor's lips parted and he blew on the tip of the cigarette. The paper sparked. Michael inhaled. Smoke poured into his lungs. "There, see? That wasn't hard."

Trying to focus with Victor's thumb curled over his chin was nearly impossible. This—Michael's flushed skin and Victor's very real, very impossible presence—felt untrue the same way guilt felt untrue. No matter how certain Michael was that he did not lean into Victor's hand, he still found more of Victor's palm on his cheek. "So, the rumors are true? Witches live in Port Lewis?"

"Witches live everywhere."

"And you…" Michael took another drag and exhaled, tipping his head back to blow the smoke at the sky. The edge of Victor's claw caught his bottom lip. His heartbeat was too fast, breath too short. Everything was too unreal. "Sold what?"

Victor hesitated. He waited for Michael to attempt another drag, then carefully pinched the cigarette and took it for himself. The lit end cast an orange glow across his face, and Michael could not look away. "I made a deal with a demon." Another long pull off the cigarette. Another press of his thumb to Michael's mouth. "Once I died, they were given access to my body and soul, and I was given access to their magic. We became one, to put it bluntly."

"How…" He caught the question before it could squirm out. *How did you die?* His bravery felt forged, because this was still impossible. This house and the smoke exhaled from Victor's mouth flowing over his lips, magic and souls that wore price tags. Impossible, he thought, but unerringly tangible.

"Interesting…" Once the tip of Victor's claw touched Michael's tongue, he pulled away, unable to suppress the sharp tug low in his stomach. A surprised grin popped open on Victor's face followed by a laugh, the good kind, honest and strong. "You let me get away with that for longer than I thought you would."

Embarrassment curled tightly in Michael's chest. "I'm not scared," he bit out. There it was again, the childish bravery that never failed to get him into trouble. "Do you do this to all your tenants? Steal their beer?" Michael wrapped his fingers over Victor's knuckles, coiled loosely around the bottleneck, and tugged it away. "Touch them without permission, and…" He had to convince his legs to move, to step backward until he was out of reach. *Haunt them.* "Fuck with them like this?"

Victor turned his smoky grin toward the sky, one thumb pushed through the belt loop on his dark jeans, cigarette balanced on the other. He stood casually, like any fucking guy in any dive bar would stand, cocky and unbothered in the face of rejection.

Mostly, because men like Victor were usually rejected as often as they were teased and teased as often as they were encouraged. Michael was accustomed to the vicious cycle, one he'd perfected and abandoned. But those were human interactions, and if Victor was telling the truth, then he'd left his human life behind. He fixed his gold eyes on Michael again, the tips of his horns skewering the light like a fitted crown of shadows, and shook his head.

"The last person who rented this house left the moment they saw me," he said calmly. "The woman before that said the space didn't have a good *vibe*. She saged the house, lit incense, opened all the windows and tried to shoo me out with the smoke." He shrugged and held the cigarette out to him. Michael took it. "I haven't spoken to anyone new in a long time."

"So, that's why you trapped me in your bedroom and said I smelled like honey." Michael's voice was barbed and sarcastic. "You were being friendly." He finished the cigarette and smothered it under his shoe. "I mean, it's no wonder those people left. I don't know if anyone's told you, but..." He inhaled sharply through his nose, skin tingling where Victor's lips had touched his neck. "Kissing someone without their permission isn't sexy, Victor. Neither is stealing their drinks or randomly manifesting in their bedroom, or—"

"Sorry to interrupt, but I just told you I sold my soul to a demon in exchange for immortality and you're upset because I took a sip off your IPA?" Victor's dark brows furrowed. He tempered his smile, awkwardly shifting from foot to foot.

Michael huffed. He sucked his cheek between his teeth and bit. Truth was, Michael wasn't afraid of Victor, but he was afraid of what Victor intended to do with him. Afraid that if he didn't speak up, Victor might slip his thumb between Michael's lips again. Afraid that if he didn't try to deter him, Victor might get a sense of what Michael really was. Intrigued.

"I didn't kiss you," Victor purred. He kept watching Michael like *that*, like he'd done this before, like seduction was as easy as an introduction.

"You..." Michael's cheeks burned hotter. "You put your..."

Night rippled, as if the air had stepped away to let Victor pass through without needing to walk. He was suddenly there, like a quick wind, hand perched on the balcony wall beside Michael's hip, mouth featherlight on his pulse.

"I put my lips here because I can taste your vitality. Your blood, your skin, the light you have inside you." Something lived under Victor's voice. Something sinister and ancient. He pressed his nose to Michael's neck and inhaled. "Your innocence smells sweet, like honey. Your energy—your *magic*—makes me hungry for a life I've left behind."

Michael's lashes fluttered. His gasp was small and fevered, voice caught in his throat. "I'm not innocent," he rasped. It was the last thing he'd wanted to say, but it was all he managed. The rest got lost between warring desires, the delirious need to press his palm to Victor's chest, to feel for a heartbeat. *There.* It pitter-pattered fast, like his own. The buttons on Victor's shirt rolled between his knuckles as he slid his hand higher, fingertips smoothing over a scar in the shape of an intricate symbol etched into his collarbone.

Victor didn't move. He stayed perfectly still, allowing Michael to touch him.

"Is this okay?" Michael asked, breathless. He traced the line of Victor's long throat, thumb trembling over his cheek, until he met the seam between skin and black bone on his temple.

"Well, look at us getting to know each other," Victor teased.

Michael leaned against the balcony wall. He placed his fingers on the base of Victor's horn and jerked back, startled to find it warm. Smooth. Entirely too touchable. He tried again, slower this time, and carefully brushed his palm along the subtle ridges and curves to the pointed tip.

Victor let out a sharp breath. "You're gentle."

Michael was disgustingly proud of himself for pulling a sound like that from a creature like him. "Not always." He closed his eyes and pushed, applying enough pressure to Victor's horn to guide him closer. He let his head tip back, thought of every time he'd chased danger and how amateur those experiences seemed in comparison.

Teeth scraped the shell of his ear. "Is this okay?"

"Don't..." Michael swallowed hard. "Just don't bite me, okay? Like, don't break skin or—"

Victor curled his arm around Michael's back, pulling until their hips knocked and his thigh was snug between Michael's legs. Lips pressed to the flexed tendon on his neck, tongue laving over freckled skin, teeth blunt and promising, barely sinking in before he pulled back to press another kiss to a different place. Michael's fingers tightened around his horn, his other hand blindly searching for a way to stay steady. He tried for the wall, then Victor's hip, his shoulder, the nape of his neck.

Somehow, Michael had found himself pinned against the edge of the balcony with his arms over Victor Lewellyn's shoulders, hands tangled in his short hair, gripping his wicked horns, being kissed on his neck and his jaw and his ear, and not once on his mouth.

Desire pooled beneath his skin wherever Victor touched. He dragged his teeth across the hinge of Michael's jaw, reached up to place a clawed hand over his knuckles, slid his thigh higher, *higher*, until Michael's gasp turned into a weak sound—a whimper he desperately tried to bite back.

"I never understood the difference between light and dark. I lived in gray, the magic that bent rules and stirred up controversy," Victor said. His nose tickled Michael's cheek as he pulled back to look at him, mouth close enough to catch if Michael lifted onto his tiptoes. "But I get it now. That shit the elders used to warn us about, how once you go without it for long enough, light becomes a rarity. Something you crave."

Michael's head swam trying to keep up. He'd believed in something—God, no. Magic, maybe. The devil, definitely—but he'd never felt suspended in something bigger than him, worse than him, darker and stranger and more powerful than him.

There was a world out there he didn't know, and he was sharing breath with one of its biggest secrets. The thought thrilled him.

"I'm not a witch, I'm not magical or filled with light or... Or anything like you," Michael said. He tried to catch his breath, to steady his inhales and exhales, and dropped his hand from Victor's horn to his cheek. "I'm just..."

"No one is *just* anything." Victor had shed the cocky exterior he'd worn before. In its place, Michael found cinders sparking in half-lidded eyes and an open, raw expression that usually accompanied shock, as if Victor was surprised by what he'd found in the hollow of Michael's throat.

He watched Victor worry his lip with his teeth, saw the way he flicked his eyes to their flush hips, and didn't break eye contact when he pressed his thigh to the place where Michael was hard and trapped and aching.

Michael's mouth quivered. Everything, *everything* narrowed down to the fit of their bodies. Darkness wrapped around them. Reality slipped from under Michael's feet. Victor's jaw slackened. He watched as Michael gathered a ratcheting breath, desire and promise written in thrumming veins and heated skin and the unbelievable idea that Victor *wanted* him.

"You taste like honey too," Victor whispered.

It was a clumsy thing at first, kissing Victor. But Michael didn't mind. He laced his fingers through Victor's hair and pulled, back arched, grinding unashamedly against his thigh. Their mouths bumped, open and gasping, before Michael curled his hand around the base of Victor's horn, angled him where he wanted, and licked into his mouth.

He tasted like cloves and bergamot.

Michael hitched his hips closer, pushing until he felt the hard line of Victor's cock between his legs.

Want was an unknown thing at a level like this. Hours ago, Michael had seen a shadow cross his floor and realized he was being haunted, and now he was sucking on the hauntee's tongue, overwhelmed and chasing an orgasm.

*Story for the books*, he thought. *At least his tongue isn't forked.*

Victor's clawed hand slid over Michael's thigh. A loud knock sounded at the front door.

"Hey! I think you have all the toothpaste!" Janice hollered.

Michael's body jolted. His hands shot back to catch the edge of the balcony wall, skin cold where Victor had been seconds ago, lips wet and knees wobbling. He sucked in uneven breaths and glanced around, looking for any sign of the household demon lurking in the dark.

No eyes caught the light. No horns punctured the moon. Just like that, he was alone again.

Another loud knock echoed through his bedroom. "Seriously, Michael? C'mon, just—"

Michael stormed through the bedroom, wrenched the door open and shoved a tube of toothpaste at her.

"Whoa, hey, you feeling okay? You're super flushed." Her brows knitted and her smile dropped into a frown.

"I'm fine, I'm just tired. Goodnight," he mumbled.

Janice stopped him from shutting the door and peeked inside. "Didn't you say you were unpacking? Because you haven't unpacked a single..." Her thin brows shot toward her hairline. "Were you masturbating? You were totally masturbating."

"Oh my fucking God, Janice, goodnight!" He placed the heel of his palm on her forehead and pushed until she finally left. Her cackles filled the hall between their rooms, followed by the sink running, the creak of a door and the flick of a light switch.

No, he'd been a few articles of clothing and a bad decision away from fucking a demon.

That's what he'd been doing.

Michael couldn't settle. Even as the minutes turned to an hour and the creaky house faded into silence, he found himself pacing, strung between hoping Victor would reappear and hoping to fall asleep and wake up in Arizona, unchanged.

He stripped off his coat then the rest of his clothes, turned the light off, and stared at the ceiling until his heartbeat calmed. Like this, Michael felt exposed. Vulnerable. Lonely, even. Because like this, sprawled on his bed in the dark, all he could think about was Victor's breath in his mouth. The black climbing from his claws into each finger. How he'd sucked on Michael's neck, and moved against him, and spoken to him.

*You taste like honey too.*

Michael replayed the phrase over and over. He bit his lip hard, reminded that alone was not *alone* in this house. That if he slid his palm across his stomach, if he wrapped his fingers around his cock, Victor could see him.

At least, that was what Michael assumed a haunting meant.

If he spread his legs and touched himself, if he pressed his thumb to the underside of his dick and gasped, if he arched his back off the bed and let his hips jump, Victor might know what he was doing—might know he was breathless and shaking and thinking of the way Victor's teeth nipped his jaw.

So, instead of indulging in the efficient, quick orgasms his hand was usually good for, Michael clutched the sheet above his head and refused to come. He loosened his grip, twisted his wrist until pleasure spiked into his legs, rubbed the liquid beading at the head of his cock in circles, and imagined it was Victor.

Victor's hand. Victor holding him down. Victor inside him. Victor's lips around his cock.

*You taste like honey too.*

Michael let out a steep breath, choking back a moan before it slipped over his lips. Chills scaled his arms and legs. Wrongness crept into the room with him. *Finally.* When he opened his eyes, a tall shadow loomed in the corner, tipped with horns. Golden flecks glinted in the dark.

*There you are.* He wanted to be touched, to wear marks down his back from Victor's claws. *Come here, please, come here.* Michael held his gaze and imagined what he might look like with moonlight gliding over his flushed skin, sweat-sheened, writhing on a bed and trying to keep his voice low.

Victor didn't move. Michael didn't stop.

He teetered on the edge, muscles flexed and body begging for release. Even though Michael wanted to draw it out, wanted to watch Victor watching him for longer, impatience won. He gasped and turned his head into his arm, biting on tender skin to muffle a soft cry he couldn't keep at bay. He dug his heels into the bed. A warm spurt landed on his hip and dripped from his fingers. Satisfaction buzzed in him, a bone-deep heat that spread into his arms and legs and knuckles and toes.

Neither of them spoke. Michael's chest rose and fell. His body sank into the bed, and his heart eased into a regular rhythm. He kept his eyes open, fixed on Victor a few feet away. The night felt like a stranger. As if the moon wore a different skin and the constellations cast a different light.

Michael knew there was no going back. He'd changed the moment he'd stepped into that house. A breath slipped out in the shape of Victor's name, but by the time he'd said it—a whispered, sore thing—he blinked, and Victor was gone.

# Part Three: Poltergeist

COREY HAD NICE teeth.

They were toothpaste-commercial white, the kind that appeared pleasantly fake the longer you looked at them. Michael hadn't expected to talk about their childhoods over brunch, but he wasn't surprised when he found out Corey's smile had been straightened from three years of uncomfortable braces, or how he came out as bisexual to his family last year, or how he'd played varsity lacrosse in high school.

Really, Michael wasn't surprised about anything Corey said, but he appreciated the normalcy nonetheless.

Last night lingered under his clothes. He'd woken to the sound of Janice sifting through wrapped glassware in the kitchen, stood in the hallway with a foamy toothbrush shoved in his mouth and stared at the attic door. The wood floors had wheezed beneath his bare feet. Wind had snapped at the windows. But the demon hadn't appeared. The door hadn't opened. After Janice left for a job interview and Victor stayed hidden, Michael looked over his shoulder as he followed Corey out the door and wondered if he'd dreamed it all.

"How early is too early for a drink?" Corey asked. A waitress stood beside their booth with a pen pressed to a notepad.

Michael glanced at Corey and lifted a brow before he said, "I'll take a double Bloody Mary, extra spicy."

"Can I see your ID, please?"

Michael flicked the plastic card out and held it between two fingers. She looked it over, looked at him, looked it over again.

"Wow, two weeks into twenty-one, huh? Happy birthday." She handed the card back and nodded to Corey. "Anything for you?"

Corey peeked at the menu and cleared his throat. "I'll take... Something, ah, I don't know, something not quite *that* strong. Whatever pale ale you have on draft is fine."

The waitress nodded and walked away.

Michael's lips cracked into a grin. "I get the feeling you were joking about that drink."

"I sorta was." His smile spoke to his nervousness, twitching up on one side more than the other. "Anyway, what were we talking about? School, right? Architecture is your thing, isn't it?"

"It's my dad's thing, and his dad's thing, and my uncle's thing." He muttered a quiet *thank you* once his drink was set in front of him then grabbed the straw and licked it clean. "I don't really have a thing."

"Everyone has a thing. C'mon." Corey was flirting the way most people did, small prods and a little bit of prying that came with curiosity. Still, Michael found it invasive.

Probably because he'd gotten no sleep. Definitely because he'd made out with a demon who might or might not be real, which meant Michael might or might not be crazy.

What happened last night made focusing on a conversation nearly impossible.

"Sorry," Corey blurted. He thumbed at the lip of his frosty glass. "That was kinda rude, I—"

"No, you're fine, I'm just tired... I didn't sleep well last night, and my fucking sister always tells people I want to get into architecture because it's the family business when she knows damn well I don't have a plan yet."

Corey was quiet for an uncomfortable amount of time. Michael licked seasoning off the rim of his glass and hissed after gulping half his drink. They ordered food. Picked at sugar packets. Made fleeting eye contact. He had to remind himself this wasn't a date, that Corey was a stranger—his roommate and potential friend. *Don't fuck this up.*

Michael raked his fingers through his hair and sipped his drink. "I like plants. My mom makes fun of me for it, but I've always been good with them. Flowers, trees, herbs, vegetables, anything that grows. Horticulture's my first choice for a major. Weird, I know."

"Weird because people in horticulture aren't usually covered in flash tattoos? Or weird because your family thinks it's the wrong choice?"

Their food came. Michael forked a fluffy piece of waffle into his mouth and rolled his eyes. "Yeah, sure. We'll go with both."

"Both it is," Corey said under his breath.

They ate quietly. Michael knew his hackles were raised. His bristles pointed outward, sharp and thick. It annoyed him that someone as sweet as Corey was on the other end of them. It was even more annoying that Michael had no good reason to be as guarded as he was. But he'd grown up with a group of friends who knew him as that, and a family who'd made him into that. He'd never known how to be anything else.

"I..." Michael heaved a sigh. *Way to go, asshole. Chase him off.* "I'm sorry, man. I'm just exhausted and freaked out. I'm a little homesick too, I guess. This whole place is super fucking weird and the house is creepy and I just...I—I got *no* sleep. None."

"It's cool." Corey dipped his last chunk of fried potato into a puddle of ketchup. "I get it. Port Lewis has a reputation. But I've never run into any warlocks or faeries or vampires—" Playfulness sparked in his cobalt eyes. "—or ghosts for that matter."

Michael remembered Victor's voice. *I can taste your vitality.* He remembered Victor's mouth on his pulse, the way he kissed like he was starving, how he disappeared in the blink of an eye.

"The house doesn't feel off to you? Not even a little bit?"

Corey shook his head. "Look, I get it. You moved here from a big city, you had a bunch of friends and went to parties and lived the life most people in small towns like these wish they had. But honestly? You're hot, you're *almost* friendly, and if you actually looked for the good in things you might find Port Lewis cozy instead of creepy."

"*Almost* friendly," Michael parroted, snorting a laugh. Corey wasn't wrong, not about the city or the friends or the parties. He was wrong in assuming they were things Michael missed.

"Speaking of where you came from... You're not the type of guy who left someone there on a promise you'd be back, are you?" Corey tested.

That kind of question was always a Trojan horse. But Corey, with his blond hair and his blue eyes, in his crisp white shirt and distressed jeans, was kind enough to believe Michael wouldn't catch on. Or he was interested enough to hope Michael would figure it out.

"I fucked a lot of people," Michael said. He watched Corey's jaw tense and his cheeks darken. "But no one in Arizona is naïve enough to think I'll ever come back for good."

Corey swallowed. His eyes darted from Michael to the table, fingers restless in his lap.

"What about you, Corey? Are you dating a Port Lewis witch?" Michael craned over the table and rolled the last word between his teeth, teasing it like a fizzled match.

"No, but if someone casts a spell on me, I'll be sure to let you know." Corey grinned again, bashful and genuine. Those white teeth. That pretty smile.

*What a pity*, Michael thought. Because even here—even with someone as perfect as Corey sitting in front of him—his skin itched for Victor.

Corey slapped the tabletop and jutted his chin toward the counter. "Come on, we'll have them split the check at the front."

Michael slid out of the booth, shrugged on his coat, and laughed to himself. There he was, swathed in a black turtleneck, torn dark washed jeans, and ratty Vans, following a walking, talking American Eagle catalog. Strange to look at a mild-mannered local with no interest in the unknown, as he remembered clutching Victor's horns, getting lost in his mouth, and staring into his eerie golden eyes.

THEY ARRIVED AT 116 Foxglove Lane precisely four minutes before the sky opened and rain splattered the town. The house was as old and tired as it had been when they left, but this time there wasn't anywhere else Michael cared to look besides the attic window. A shadow bent, as if someone had drawn a line down the glass. The curtains whispered, caught by a breeze or a breath.

A raindrop hit his forehead. Another wet his cheek. Another and another. He watched for claws or broad shoulders, but no one appeared.

"You coming?" Corey stood in the doorway with his keys in his hand.

Michael nodded, reluctantly tearing his eyes from the window high above the porch. "Thanks for today," he said. He shrugged off his coat and toed the door shut, pacing into the kitchen after Corey. "I had a good time. We should..."

Corey's keys clattered on the tile floor.

No reaction would appropriately convey the many layers of Michael's irritation. Not because he hadn't expected it, but because he knew that no matter what he said or what he'd seen, Corey and Janice would not believe him.

The four wooden chairs that matched their rickety round breakfast table were haphazardly stacked on the tabletop. Across from the table, the kitchen was awkwardly upended. Every drawer had been pulled out. Every cabinet door opened. The grates on the stove were all flipped upside down, and the empty beer bottles from last night had been arranged in a perfect line across the counter.

"Holy shit..." Corey grabbed his keys off the floor by his feet.

There was absolutely nothing holy about this. Michael sighed. At least he wasn't crazy.

"Your sister probably did this, huh? To mess with you?"

"I doubt she could get those chairs stacked like that." Michael flicked his wrist toward the topsy-turvy furniture arrangement.

"Okay, but she's the only other person with a key."

Michael sighed through his nose.

"You seriously think it was a ghost?"

"Ghost? No," Michael said matter-of-factly. He walked into the kitchen and pushed the drawers into place, closed the cabinets, arranged the stove appropriately. "Maybe something else, though."

"Something like your sister," Corey deadpanned.

"If that makes you feel better about it, then yeah, sure."

"What *do* you think it was?"

"Probably the malevolent spirit who lives in the attic." Michael didn't bother dulling the bite in voice. The words carried, echoing through the house. He added, "Or our landlord," as sarcastically as possible.

Corey let out an exasperated laugh. "You're *totally* right." Michael paused, bottle necks snug between his knuckles, and closed his eyes. "It was probably our landlord just pranking us. I mean, Port Lewis is like, known for being weird and haunted. I bet she does this to all her tenants."

Michael didn't get the chance to roll his eyes, because as soon as Corey finished his sentence, a door on the second floor slammed.

He startled and the bottles clanked. Corey nearly jumped out of his skin.

"Must've left a window open," Corey blurted, but his white skin and dilated pupils said otherwise.

"You sure about that?" He leaned past the wall dividing the kitchen from the staircase and glanced at the landing on the second floor.

"You know what? Fuck this. I'm gonna go study at Starbucks. Feel free to tell your sister or our landlord or whoever the hell is messing with us that we both laughed hysterically, okay? Or call a priest. Whichever."

"Corey, come on, it's—"

"Nope. I'm out. See you tonight," he said. Corey offered him a thin, pained smile as he walked by, grabbed his messenger bag, and was out the door a second later.

*Great.* Michael dropped the bottles in the recycling bin. He glared at the ceiling and shook his head. "Are you proud of yourself?" he called to the empty house. Rain streaked the windows and bounced off the roof. Victor didn't answer. "This is why you have no friends," he hollered, walking in a circle, gaze dragging from one end of the ceiling to the other. "You scare them off!"

The house creaked and shifted, but nothing appeared and no one shouted back to him.

Michael tidied the kitchen. He tried to unstack the chairs from atop the table and they toppled over, creating a loud, heavy mess. One whacked his shoulder as it fell. Another landed on his foot. Annoyance blistered in him. He cracked his knuckles and shoved the chairs into place.

Once things were back where they belonged, he unpacked the two boxes Janice hadn't gotten to. Dishes went in one cabinet. Wineglasses and shot glasses in another. He organized until he felt better, until embarrassing replays of breakfast with Corey—his abrasive attitude and callous unapproachability—waned. Until Michael had almost pushed the thought of Victor to the wayside, until he almost felt at ease.

An hour passed. Another. The rain got worse and storm clouds rolled in from the sea. But at least the couch was situated against the wall and the coffee table was wiped down. A flat-screen TV hung above the fireplace. Their waffle iron was tucked neatly next to the toaster between the blender and the fridge.

He wiped his forehead with the back of his hand. "There," he said out loud, filling the space with noise now that he'd stopped for long enough to notice the silence.

Upstairs, his room was unchanged. Boxes still littered the ground. Some drawers were empty; others were half-filled with folded clothes. He opened the door that led to the balcony and left it ajar, trying not to dwell on the memory of being pressed against the short wall a few feet away, panting and breathless, with Victor between his legs.

A text came through as he lit a cigarette.

JANICE: *Me and Corey are going to trivia night at the brewery downtown. You in?*
MICHAEL: *Theme?*
JANICE: *Harry Potter*
MICHAEL: *No thanks. I still need to unpack.*
JANICE: *Watch out for phantoms ;)*

A shadow dripped from the ceiling, so quick he might not have noticed if Victor's voice didn't accompany it. "That was quite a show you put on last night."

The cigarette sparked when he took a long drag, but neither the nicotine nor the headrush did anything to calm the stutter in his chest or the heat in his cheeks. "You scared the hell out of my roommate with your poltergeist bullshit."

"He wasn't *that* scared."

Michael's eyes narrowed.

Victor leaned against the wall with his arms folded across his chest. The only simple thing about him was his attire. A gray shirt. Straight-legged jeans. But the rest was still complicated. Still terrifying. Still powerful and alluring.

"Did you have a good time on your date?" Victor asked.

"It wasn't a date." He tossed his phone on the bed and set his shoulder against the door, trying and failing to stay composed. Victor was within reach. Michael wasn't sure if he was breathing. *Did he even need to breathe?* Questions crowded his throat, so many, too many. "That kitchen table set was our grandma's," he bit out. "Don't mess with it again."

Victor arched a dark brow. "Look at you," he cooed. "Like a Halloween cat. Ears pinned. Teeth bared. You're adorable."

"Seriously." Michael's voice lowered. He blew smoke through the crack in the door. "We literally put our handprints in paint on the bottom of it when we were babies. Our mom would kill us if it broke right after we got permission to use it."

The smile on Victor's face softened. His lips parted, but he didn't say anything, just looked at Michael skeptically, head tilted and shoulders loose. Slowly, Victor lifted his hand from its place on his elbow and held out two fingers, asking for the cigarette.

Michael handed it to him. "Finish it." He stole another glance at Victor's sculpted face before he walked into the hall. It was an off-putting sensation, turning his back on a demon. He didn't know what to expect. Victor was playful and confident; he smoked cigarettes and drank beer and had a nice laugh.

But he also had claws. And horns. And shared his body with another entity.

*Everyone has baggage.* Michael almost laughed at himself. Almost. He turned on the shower, stripped, and closed the glass door behind him.

*That was quite a show you put on last night.*

Michael's whole body flushed. He swallowed and turned the knob to the right. The water heated, stinging his freckled shoulders. He watched Victor's shape appear on the other side of the glass door, his horns blurred, silhouette misshapen by the steam.

"How old were you when you died?" Michael asked.

"Twenty-eight. How old are you?"

"Twenty-one."

"You're a baby," Victor said, surprised.

Michael bit back a laugh. "My parents wouldn't agree with you. I should be graduating next year," he mocked, "and helping with the family business, and I shouldn't have wasted all that time traveling, because what will seeing the world get you? Nothing." He heaved a sigh. "What'll being happy get you? Definitely not a livable income," he added under his breath.

Victor tilted his head. "Where'd you go?"

Having a conversation was easier like this. Michael didn't actually have to look at him, and more importantly, Michael didn't actually have to be looked at. He didn't have to be seen. "I started in Denmark. Went to Spain, Germany... Bounced over to London and then went to Belgium and Italy."

"I've always wanted to see the Vatican," Victor said.

"You wouldn't burst into flames?"

Victor's laugh was honest and effortless. "Doubt it. Did you see the catacombs in Paris?"

"Course. And ate fancy cheese under the Eiffel Tower, smoked weed in Amsterdam, took a selfie at Stonehenge. I did it all."

"But did you have sex in a hostel?" Victor asked. There was something young about his charm, something warm and lonesome.

Michael grinned and closed his eyes. "A couple times. When's the last time you slept with someone?"

"That's not a very fair question since I've been trapped in this house for a year."

"Then I'm the first tenant you've successfully seduced?"

"I was successful?"

Michael bit down hard on his bottom lip, smiling through it. "How come you're trapped here?"

"This is where I made the bond with Allocer. It's complicated."

"Allocer..." Michael tested the name on his tongue. He watched Victor's shape straighten, listened to his breath catch. "There's power in names, isn't there? For demons or—"

"Careful, Michael."

Michael exhaled a sharp breath. Hot water hit his back, the nape of his neck, the top of his head. "How'd you die?"

Everything halted. The air stood still. Even the water paused, warping like an old movie. Lights flickered and doors trembled. Caution twisted through the room.

Victor didn't answer. He pushed off the vanity and stepped closer to the shower. His palm slid over the glass, dark, bony fingers curved into points where his claws sprouted from each nailbed. Michael placed his hand on the glass too. Like this, they were vague—edges softened by the steam. He wondered what Victor saw through the glass, if he could see the tattoos on Michael's arms and neck, in the hollow beneath his hipbones and etched into his inner thighs.

Michael's lips grazed the glass, creating a sliver of clarity through the fog.

Very quietly, Victor said, "The last person I slept with is the same person who killed me."

Breath caught in his throat. Water dripped off his eyelashes. The truth was awful like this. Unexpected. Michael wanted to rewind the conversation. He wanted to go back to the laughter, to the excitement building in his chest, to Victor's playful voice and wry smile.

"I'm sorry," he said because he didn't know what else to say.

Victor hummed. His hand followed Michael's, dragging slowly down the glass, revealing thin, long strips of skin. "Did you know I was watching you last night?"

Michael pressed his palm to the glass. Bits of his stomach showed. His collarbone. Half his face. He flicked his gaze from where their hands were divided by the glass to Victor's golden eyes. He nodded. "Should I be afraid of you?"

"I wouldn't hurt you." His brows furrowed. Michael saw the way his throat flexed, as if he'd caught himself in a lie. "I wouldn't hurt you on purpose," he corrected.

"But you could?"

Victor set his forehead against the shower door. His horns clanked the glass. "Yeah, I could," he whispered.

"Do you want to?"

He rolled his bottom lip between his teeth and closed his eyes. Victor looked awkwardly human like this, stuck between the truth and an acceptable answer. "No," he said. "Not unless you want me to."

What a vicious thing power turned into when it was framed as simply as that—given to Michael in a span of six words. *Not unless you want me to.* He tracked Victor's movements, the way his eyes locked onto his face and then drifted across his bare chest, how his hand fell from the glass, and his chin lifted. He walked away after a quick glance over his shoulder, and Michael listened to the steps creak, the hinges on the attic door whine, and let his weight fall into the shower wall as the door clicked shut.

Secrets festered in this house. Magic and darkness and memories that Michael had no business trying to understand. But Victor *lived* in this house, and Michael knew he wouldn't be able to shake him. Not after yesterday. Not after last night. Not after any of this.

Michael Gates was reckless and brave. He was lonely and guarded and haunted.

*This is a bad idea,* he thought. *If you go into his room, you won't come out the same.*

But Michael scrubbed his skin with soap scented like fig and vanilla. He washed his hair and brushed his teeth and knew his mind had been made up since the moment he'd seen Victor for the first time. Even when he rubbed a fresh towel over his skin, he couldn't stop trembling. Even when he hesitated, pacing back and forth in front of the mirror in a pair of sweats and nothing else. Even when he chewed on his thumbnail and noticed the flush building in his chest and cheeks. Even when he nodded to his reflection, feigning the slightest bit of confidence, and made for the steps at the end of the hall.

*Everything changes after this.*

Everything had already changed.

The door was cool beneath his palm, already unlocked. He took a deep breath, allowing the excitement and nervousness and the tiniest bit of disbelief to push his heart into overdrive. Thunder rattled the roof.

The attic bedroom was lit by a dim lamp on the nightstand. Michael curled his hand around the edge of the door and hovered there, watching lightning streak across the dark, gray sky past the window. Rain kept falling, wind kept whistling, and Victor stood with his fingers twisted lightly through the lace curtain, gaze fixed on the same sky and the same storm.

Michael closed the bedroom door. He twisted the lock for good measure. "Victor," he said, keeping his voice even, his breath steady.

Victor's chin tipped over his shoulder. His hair was short enough to look good like that, messy and unkempt, and just long enough to tangle around Michael's fingers. He took a step and crossed the room in one breath. Oxygen crawled away from them, disrupted by Victor's magic. Dark wisps floated around his horns like smoke, fading as the air tilted back into place.

"I can't glamour myself for long," Victor said. His eyes flicked around Michael's face. He eased his weight from one foot to the other and his tongue darted out to wet his lips. "But I will if you want me to. I can make myself look like I did last night when I showed you—"

"You don't have to do that," Michael said.

He was suddenly aware of the exposed ink on his skin. How low his sweats were situated on his hips. How lightning illuminated the edge of Victor's cheekbones.

"Where can I touch you?" Victor trailed his fingers over Michael's stomach, fleeting but deliberate.

Michael's breath caught. He shook his head. *Wherever you want.* "You don't..." His eyes slipped shut and he leaned into the drag of Victor's claws over his ribs.

"I'll tell you to stop if I want to. Don't"—a breath gusted from him, stolen by Victor's mouth close to his cheek, under his ear, on his neck—"don't leave marks where people will see and don't..." His hand found Victor's jaw and curled around the back of his head, bringing them closer. "You can bite me, just don't—"

"Blood is a powerful thing." Victor's lips pressed against his pulse. "I wouldn't take yours unless you offered it to me."

"Okay," he whispered. His fingers tangled in Victor's hair. "Okay," he said again and tugged until their cheeks brushed and their noses bumped, until he could tilt his head and catch Victor's mouth in a hard kiss.

Hot breath stuttered in Michael's mouth. Victor kissed aggressively at first, prying at Michael's lips, working his jaw as he pressed him into the door, forcing his head to tilt back and his grip to tighten. A low, eager sound bubbled in Michael's throat. He waited until their kisses slowed to frame Victor's face in his hands. His thumbs followed the sharp bones beneath his skin, brushed over his eyebrows and fit around the base of his horns. They could've stayed like that for hours—Victor's tongue rubbing slowly against his own, his teeth nipping Michael's bottom lip.

But he wanted more. He wanted Victor's skin against his.

Michael broke away to breathe. He dropped his hands to fumble with Victor's jeans, fingers urgent and clumsy on two buttons—*who the fuck wears jeans with two buttons?*—and a stubborn zipper. Victor's eyes were half-lidded, golden irises dancing like lit candle wicks.

"Can I touch you?" Michael let bravery guide him. He kissed the corner of Victor's lips, the edge of his jaw, sucked and mouthed at his throat.

Victor's head lolled. He ran his hands along Michael's spine, curled them around his hips and pulled. "If you want to."

"Do *you* want me to?" He followed Victor step for step. His fingertips pressed against the soft skin stretched between his hipbones just above the line of his unbuttoned jeans. Once they found the bed, Victor was quick to push Michael onto the rumpled comforter.

The action gave him pause, the slightest bit of caution. Victor glanced at the lamp on the nightstand and it went out. A hot blush tinted Michael's cheeks and his throat and his chest, and grew darker as he watched Victor pull his shirt off and toss it to the floor.

Victor's body matched the rest of him. His collarbones were too pronounced. He wasn't overly muscular, but he was bigger than Michael, with a wide chest tapering down to jutting hipbones. *He looks like temptation*, Michael thought. Something the devil would dangle to instigate desire instead of doubt.

A square made of four crosses scarred his chest. It was a dark mark over his heart, drawn with the precision of a razor blade. A fifth cross cut the square down the middle and runes decorated the corners of the symbol. Michael placed one hand over the scar and slid his other down Victor's stomach until his fingertips dipped under the edge of his jeans. He waited, fixed on the part of Victor's lips, the catch in his breath.

"Yes, I want you to," Victor whispered. His palms were on either side of Michael's shoulders. Knees bracketed his hips. He kissed deeply, tongue dipping into Michael's mouth, riding the ridge of his teeth.

He didn't know why he assumed Victor wouldn't be wearing boxers, but he was surprised when he slid his hand into Victor's jeans and found fabric instead of skin. Victor's breathing quickened. He sucked Michael's bottom lip between his teeth and bit, tugging on it as he pulled back, placing wet, open kisses on his neck and his shoulder. Heat followed every movement. Victor's lips met black ink on Michael's sternum—an Atlas moth spread over the top of his stomach.

Michael removed his hand from inside Victor's jeans and pushed his fingers through his hair instead. Teeth dug into Michael's ribs. His back arched off the bed, breath ragged and loud. It hurt and it didn't. Being bitten. Feeling bruises bloom under his skin. Victor crept lower. Michael closed his eyes and tried to ignore the self-conscious prang in his chest. His body wasn't sculpted, but his stomach was flat and soft, toned from yoga and running. Lean wasn't always at the top of people's preference list. Neither was bony. Or scarred. Or freckled. Really, he hadn't cared about what people preferred until Victor was the one on top of him.

Victor's knees hit the floor. He opened his mouth over the three lines on Michael's hip, sucking the short scars between his teeth. A tattoo covered them—a scorpion. Hands curled under his thighs, higher, over his ass to the band of his sweats. The sharp point of Victor's claws dug in, stinging their way down again, across the supple skin on his backside. Michael's sweats went with them, pushed to his thighs, his shins, the ground.

"Not fair," Michael said. His voice came out winded. Too soft.

Victor's low laugh was the only answer he got. Then it was his mouth on Michael's inner thigh, a sharp bite to the skin there, his lips parting, tongue in the junction where his hip met his leg. He sucked marks on Michael's hips and thighs, flattened his hands over his waist and held him down, and finally, after Michael was whimpering and squirming, wrapped his lips around Michael's cock.

Heat pooled low in his stomach. This was pleasure he had no language for. The hot stroke of Victor's tongue, how he relaxed his jaw and took him deeper, *deeper*, until his throat fluttered and he pulled back.

"Fuck, do that again," Michael said.

He wasn't necessarily expecting Victor to do as he was told, but he did—lips parted, tongue hot and wet, curling around the head of Michael's cock. Victor hummed and swallowed around him, easing himself closer, pushing until his nose grazed Michael's pelvis. His mouth was slick. Lips messy. He swallowed again, throat flexing and jumping.

Michael's back bowed, hands urgent and impatient, landing on Victor's jaw, his shoulders, then clutching his horns. He hadn't imagined panting and trembling, crying out as Victor's teeth grazed the base of his cock. He hadn't considered that Victor might take his time. Might dig his claws into the skin stretched between his hipbones. Might flinch and moan whenever Michael pulled on him. Might push Michael's legs apart and hollow his cheeks and be this good.

But Victor's mouth was *so* warm, too warm, unnaturally warm. His claws left mean, red trails down Michael's thighs. When he pulled back to gather a breath, Michael fumbled to get a better grip on his horns and tugged him into a kiss. His lips were slick and sticky, tongue flavored like come and black tea.

"I wasn't done," Victor mumbled. He held himself above Michael, hands on either side of him. His knees eased back onto the bed.

"You're still not done." Michael tilted his head to accommodate another long, lingering kiss. He pushed at Victor's jeans with his feet then let go of his horns for long enough to reach down and shove his briefs away too.

The rest of their clothes dropped to the floor. He glanced between them, unsure of what he might find. Which was ridiculous. Victor could almost pass as human. If it weren't for the black bone curving from his temples, his claws and gorgeous eyes, he might be able to deceive people into believing he was just… Michael looked at Victor's broad, round shoulders, his strong arms and the scar on his chest. *Maybe not.* He wrapped his fingers around Victor's cock. His skin was smooth and dark, heavy in his palm and entirely normal.

"You look surprised," Victor teased. His breath gave him away, held too tight when he spoke and let out too fast when he didn't.

Michael's eyes flicked to his horns. He stroked Victor slowly, watching the way his abdomen twitched and his lashes fluttered. "How long can you…" He couldn't remember the word. "Your claws," he blurted, and let go of Victor's cock to grab his hips. He arched off the bed and rolled against him. "How are we gonna do this?"

"How long can I what, and what about my claws?"

Sex wasn't usually this complicated. He chewed on his lip, considering. Then he took Victor's hand and brought it to his face. The black tips of his fingers touched his chin. His lips parted and he held Victor's gaze, guiding two fingers into his mouth.

Victor's knuckles bent. He dragged the pointed tip of his elongated fingernails across his tongue and stayed still when Michael sucked on them. His fingers were long. Michael imagined them elsewhere—inside him—rubbing and curling.

"Do you trust me?" Victor asked. He slid his wet fingers away, dragging them down Michael's throat. As soon as Michael nodded, Victor sat up. "Turn around."

Being vulnerable was not Michael's strong suit. Neither was being exposed. Like this, laid bare, hard and wanting and on display, he suddenly wished it was darker. He wanted the storm to black out the sky. He wanted lightning to stop flashing and the rain to hit the window harder. Victor opened the nightstand drawer. Michael shifted until his cheek was on his folded arms, unsure if he should close his legs or slide under the comforter.

The bed dipped. Victor crawled closer, eased his knees apart, and kissed his calf. His lips climbed the back of Michael's leg, mouth tender on his thigh, teeth harsh on the top of his ass. Thunder rumbled again.

"I like this one." Victor pressed another kiss to the old, poorly drawn crow's skull tattooed on his shoulder.

"It was my first." Michael closed his eyes and lifted his hips, thighs trembling as he slid his knees further apart. Breath hit the nape of his neck. Victor's slick fingers dipped between his legs. "I won't break," he said and pressed back against him. "Don't go slow."

"You're not very good at letting people take care of you," Victor said.

Michael tilted his head to look at Victor. He meant to bite something back at him. To tell him not to fuck around, to do something already, to hurry up. But two of Victor's fingers pressed inside him, blunt and bony and perfect, and silenced anything he'd planned to say. He squeezed his eyes shut, mouth open, gathering fractured, heavy breaths.

Victor didn't listen. He took his time. The heel of his palm met the top of Michael's ass, fingers deep, and he circled his wrist, rubbing and stroking. A kiss between his shoulder blades coupled with Victor's deft fingers brought Michael too close to the edge for comfort. He muffled a moan against his arm and twisted the sheets in a white-knuckled grip. Pleasure sparked inside him. Whimpers dissolved into barely there sounds that Michael would've been ashamed of had he been in anyone else's bed.

"Easy." Victor's voice verged on apprehensive. He paused and took a breath, easing a third digit beside the first two.

Michael's toes curled. He tried to stay still but his hips jerked and his spine bent. He pushed into Victor's hand, searching for more of him.

Emptiness was a sudden thing. Victor's fingers were gone. He growled, frustrated and inhuman—words razor-sharp against Michael's neck. "You can't distract me when I'm casting," he snapped. "Glamour isn't easy." He rubbed his fingers over Michael's hole again, tipped with claws he'd spelled away seconds ago.

Chills scaled Michael's arms and legs. "Fine, I get it. Just…" He lifted his hips again, grinding his ass into Victor's thighs, higher, *higher*, until Victor's cock slid against him.

Michael gasped. He felt Victor's hand on his hip, tugging, then he was on his back, palms on Victor's face, pulling him into a kiss. His hip burned, warm and wet where Victor's claw had torn his skin. He didn't pay attention to the pain. It was overshadowed by Victor's body, by his mouth on Michael's mouth, his arms under Michael's thighs, the weight of his cock inside him.

"Fuck, you okay?" Victor stopped and covered the mark on Michael's hip with a shaking palm. When he lifted his hand, a tiny bit of blood streaked his skin.

Irritation immediately lurched into Michael's throat. He wanted to hiss again. *Of course I'm okay.* To swat the regret off Victor's face. *Come back, don't stop.* He nodded instead and looped his arms over Victor's shoulders, closing the space between them.

Blood from Victor's hand turned the sheets beside his head bright red. He gripped Michael's thigh with the other, holding him carefully, claws barely pressed to his flesh. Michael's hips jumped. He met Victor's movements, listening to their breath fill the empty room, to Victor moan against his mouth. Rain peppered the window. Lightning struck again. A white flash stretched over them and the bed and the bloody sheets.

Michael said his name on a weak breath.

Victor gripped harder. His teeth sank into Michael's shoulder—sharper, deeper. His carefulness dissolved into hard snaps of his hips, a ruthless pace. Pleasure jolted into Michael's bones and lungs and wet his lashes.

This was intimacy Michael didn't know. It was a brutal kind of sensuality and it made him careless. He raked his nails across Victor's shoulders, let his head tip back and gasped, voice steeper, eyes closed. His orgasm unfurled quickly, a heat that released and pulsed inside him, climbing higher with every rock of Victor's hips. Michael squirmed and cried out. He tried to catch his breath, thighs tightening around Victor's waist, back arched, neck long and lips parted.

He'd been with a lot of people, he'd been a lot of places, but nothing had ever been like this.

Michael clung to Victor through the aftershocks. He was oversensitive, wrung out, and deeply satisfied. He tangled his fingers in the short hair behind Victor's horns and bit down hard on his neck. Claws almost pierced the skin on his thigh. *Almost.* But Victor moved his hand before they could, grabbing Michael's ribs instead, pushing him down, hard, *harder*, until his hips stuttered and he came, gasp accompanied by a quiet, raspy moan.

After, the room fell into comfortable quiet. Their breathing filled the empty space, fast then slow. Michael touched Victor's chest, his sides, trailed his fingers over his shoulders and neck, littered with bruises and bite marks.

Victor looked at him. His cheeks were flushed, lips still wet and swollen. He leaned into Michael's hand on his jaw, and kissed him gently, slowly. "You okay?"

He was sore and quivering and unhinged. But he couldn't think of a way to explain that without sounding *not* okay. "Yeah, are you?"

"You sure?" He dragged his thumb over Michael's cheek and rested it at the corner of his eye, still wet from a stray, bothersome tear.

"It wasn't a sentimental thing," Michael said. He couldn't help the honesty that crept into his voice, even if each word came out rasped and raw. "I'm fine. You just..."

"What?"

*Changed me.* "I'm fine," he said again. "Could probably use a Band-Aid though."

Victor eased back. Michael's mouth tightened and his lashes fluttered when he pulled out. He masked the flinch with a smirk, swallowing the urge to cover himself, to hide under the sheets. Come splattered his stomach. His thighs were damp, remnants of Victor still fresh and hot inside and around him. Usually, he'd already be in the bathroom, cleaning up, forgetting names, thinking of an escape route. But this time he stayed. This time he let Victor look at him.

Lightning flashed and Victor was gone. A moment later footsteps hit the steps in the hall. The locked doorknob jostled. An irritated sigh came from the other side of the door, then in the span of a quick breath, Victor was there again, manifesting from the shadows.

The Band-Aid was pale blue, dotted with tiny yellow suns. "We should probably shower first," Victor said, his thoughtfulness timid but endearing.

"Remember yesterday, when you told me I smelled like honey and I thought you were gonna eat me," Michael blurted. His head was still fuzzy. Body still reeling. He bit back a soft laugh, grin loose and easy.

Victor crawled over him on his hands and knees. "I could still eat you." He kissed a new bruise on his hip, another on his ribcage. "I probably will."

"Fuck you," Michael said through a bout of laughter. He closed his eyes at the touch of Victor's lips to his pulse. "Do you sleep?"

"I don't think I have to, but yeah. Habit, I guess."

"Do you eat food?"

"*What?*" Victor stretched out beside him, elbow propped, head resting on his closed fist. "Yes, I eat food. I do laundry too. Why?"

"You just said you don't think you have to sleep. Don't act shocked because I asked if you actually eat." Another surprised laugh hiccupped in Michael's throat. "What's it like when you…" He didn't know how to say it. "When you manifest like that?"

"Sometimes I don't even realize I'm doing it." He rolled his eyes and heaved a sigh. "I'll want to be somewhere, or I'll hear something and want to know where it came from, or imagine peeking into someone's bedroom, and then"—he shrugged—"I'm there."

"But you can't see through walls or anything?"

"No."

"And you can't leave the house?"

"Not yet, no."

"And your mom knows you're here?"

"Yes."

"But she still rents the house out to people?"

"Obviously."

Michael's brow furrowed. His grin widened and he shook his head. "And then you scare them away?"

"By accident, usually. I've been on my own for a while." The last bit snuck out quickly, quieter and lonelier than the rest. He reached out and placed his palm on Michael's cheek. "Haven't done *this* in a while—ever, actually."

"Fucked a guy after knowing him for two days?"

"Fucked a human after becoming something else." Victor's eyes were easy to get lost in. They were too black in the center, rimmed in bright, burning gold. This close, Michael could spot the movement, like solar flares constantly undulating from his pupil. Victor pressed his cheek into the pillow, a tender movement attached to things Michael still wasn't used to—comfort, closeness, affection.

"You're not very different," Michael said. He touched Victor's knuckles, curled delicately over his cheek, then dragged his fingers to the scar on his chest. "What's this?"

"Allocer's sigil." Victor dropped his hand to Michael's hip and traced the scars there, then moved to his forearm, his ribcage. They were everywhere, lines drawn by a shaky hand when Michael had felt too much and not enough, covered by ink and hidden until touched. "What're these?"

"Just old scars." They were much more than that.

Victor met his gaze. He didn't ask again, but Michael saw the curiosity in his eyes. Before he could find a way to frame the question—*Why would you do that to yourself? What happened? Do you still…?*—Michael kissed him. He gripped Victor's face and stroked his cheek with his thumb, followed the seam of skin dividing his temple from his horn. They traded breath for a long time. It was the kind of making out Michael rarely engaged in. Profoundly simple. The kind that felt good and wasn't rushed, paired with wandering hands and stolen glances.

Red lights flashed behind Michael's eyes. Sirens rang in his chest. *Oh no, you idiot.* Victor pulled back and their noses brushed. *Look what you've done.*

Victor Lewellyn was demonic and haunting, magical and intimidating. But Michael wasn't afraid of him because of that.

"Shower?" Victor asked.

Michael Gates had caught *feelings*. And that was certainly worse.

# Part Four: History

MICHAEL WAS VERY good at very few things. He was a talented writer. On occasion, he could cook. Beer pong? No competition. But his true talent was barely qualifiable as a talent at all because there wasn't much skill involved. Or practice. Or training.

Plants just happened to like him, and he just happened to like them back.

"Is it hard?" Corey asked. He held a woven basket in one hand and kept a ladder sturdy with the other.

Michael stood on the top step of the ladder, screwing a metal hook into the ceiling. "Is what hard?"

"Keeping them alive."

"Not really." He took the rope attached to the caladium's basket and secured it through the hook. "They just take time, I guess. Lots of people tell me their plants always die on them and I never understand why. They're the easiest shit in the world to take care of."

It'd been three days since Michael slept with Victor. His boxes were finally unpacked. Photographs were stuck to a corkboard on the wall. A yoga mat was neatly tucked in the corner and books filled the shelves beside his bed.

Three days since he'd been in Victor's bed for the first time. Two days since he'd laughed his way around an awkward discussion about their household ghost. *No, no, Corey was right, it was probably just the landlord. No, I haven't noticed anything weird since. Yes, Janice, I'm sure.* One day since Corey had pitched the idea of a housewarming party.

"Thanks for helping me with these," Michael said.

Three baskets hung from hooks in the ceiling, crowded with green vines and wide leaves that draped over their edges. A larger pot was seated in the corner by the dresser, home to an Alocasia with giant dark leaves veined white in the center. There was a bushy fern on his nightstand. A massive bundle of Plantain Lilies lazed on the shady side of the balcony, and a row of succulents in small clay pots decorated the balcony wall.

Somehow, the house that reeked of wrongness a few days ago was beginning to feel like home.

Corey folded the ladder. Their eyes met and he offered a smile. "So, Janice is down for the party. What about you?"

"If you guys want to, I mean, I don't have any friends in town or anything, but I'll pitch in for beer."

"I have friends. They're a rowdy group, though. I bet a few of them will try to get in here," Corey said. His smile parted into a grin, showcasing all his perfect teeth, and his perfect dimples, and his ridiculous straight nose.

Returning that smile would probably land him in flirtatious waters, and if there was anything worse than sleeping with the demon who lived in the attic, it would definitely be sleeping with his roommate. Michael offered a small smile back. Confusion formed a shallow line between his brows.

"In here," Corey clarified, jutting his chin toward Michael's bed. "I told them not to be dicks about it, but I doubt they'll listen."

"Dicks about what?"

Corey's blue eyes wandered from Michael's feet to his face, a slow, deliberate once-over.

Michael swallowed hard. *Oh*. Heat tinted his cheeks. "That's... I'm—I mean—I'm sure your friends are cool." The tops of his ears burned. "But I'm sort of..."

"Don't tell me you're off the market," Corey joked. His eyes crinkled when he laughed, head tilted over his shoulder as he carried the ladder through the doorway. "Because from what I remember, no one in Arizona is waiting for you. Right?"

"Right," Michael said.

"Good. Then I'll let everyone know we're down for Saturday night."

"Yeah, awesome, great," he blurted. Corey was already around the corner, ladder banging on the wall as he went, and probably, *thankfully*, didn't hear the dread in Michael's voice. Not that he wasn't flattered—he was—and not that he didn't love a good party—he definitely did.

But because he knew this house was steeped in something darker than Corey or Janice could imagine. And maybe, possibly, because he'd spent the last three days kissing that darkness.

He plucked a cigarette from the pack on his nightstand and walked onto the balcony. Bitter air nipped at his hands and cut through his sweater, a slouchy, moth-eaten disaster he refused to throw away. The holes in his jeans killed any potential insulation and he probably should've put shoes on, but at least the air was clean, scented like forest and the sea.

Smoke leaked from between his lips. He felt the air shift. Breath hit his nape and suddenly there was a warm, broad chest snug against his back.

"Did you shut the door?" Michael blew smoke at the ground. Victor's toes twitched next to his heels.

The bedroom door creaked, floating across the floor on its own. Once it closed, the lock twisted.

A tight-lipped laugh hummed in Michael's throat. He didn't know if he would ever get used to this. To this house, to magic, to Victor's lips on his neck. He didn't know if he would ever get tired of Victor wandering into the shower with him or going down on him in the kitchen when no one was home or appearing on the balcony to keep him warm while he indulged in bad habits.

Victor's mouth grazed his ear. "Will you have dinner with me tonight?"

"I would if I wasn't already going out with Janice."

"Dessert?"

Effortless, irritating excitement flapped in Michael's chest. *Butterflies* was an adequate description for a crush. But using them to describe how he felt with Victor seemed ridiculous. These were bats inside him. Or hawks. Or vultures. He lifted the cigarette back to his lips and took another drag. "It's too cold for ice cream."

"It's not too cold for brownies," Victor said matter-of-factly.

"Brownies, huh? Isn't there a prince of Hell living inside you?"

"That doesn't mean I don't like brownies." Victor kissed the underside of his jaw. "It just means I can't ask you to go *out*-out with me."

Michael hadn't asked about the demonic bond keeping Victor locked inside the house. He hadn't asked about the person who killed him either. He'd been too busy leaning against the shower door, palms flat against the glass, panting and moaning with Victor grinding into him. Or clutching black horns as he arched off the couch, mouth open and head tipped back, Victor's fingers deep inside him, mouth hot between his legs. Or on his knees with claws pushed through his hair, pressing wet, messy kisses along Victor's cock.

The last three days had been eventful.

"Do any of your friends ever come see you?" Michael asked. He rested the back of his head on Victor's shoulder.

"They did in the beginning, but then the Lewellyn matriarch put her foot down." He shrugged, hands drifting under the hem of Michael's sweater. "Elemental witches don't mingle with demonic entities. Especially when a demon's energy merges with a witch's magic. Attachment? That's one thing. What I am is completely different."

"I have no idea what any of that means."

Victor took the cigarette and set it between his lips. "Attachment happens when someone allows an entity to harness their energy. It's a give-and-take type of thing." He exhaled smoke through his nose. "I gave Allocer access to my soul in exchange for something—"

"Eternal life," Michael said.

"Yeah, in layman's terms, eternal life." Victor handed the cigarette back to him. "The difference between attachment and integration isn't a hop, skip and a jump. It's massive. One, because attachment is less invasive than integration, two, because integration means I don't just share a body with Allocer, I share my soul with him. We're not separated by will or consciousness."

"And people who form *attachments* with things like Allocer are still considered witches?"

Victor nodded.

Michael stretched his arm toward the balcony wall and dropped the cigarette in a damp ashtray. "But you're not?"

Victor nodded again. "Attachment is a partnership. Integration is an evolution."

The neighborhood was quiet. Tall trees hugged the fence and car tires shushed through puddles on the road leading into town. They weren't quite close enough to see the ocean, but Michael could still smell it. Brine and sand. He felt it on his skin, salty, dry air that made Port Lewis seem wild and rugged. Undiscovered.

"So, all your friends wrote you off? Just like that?"

Victor sighed. "Magic complicates things."

"How?"

"I like your new plants." Victor's attempt to change the subject was obvious and poorly executed. Michael smiled anyway. "Were they shipped from back home?"

"A couple were. The lilies over there." He pointed to the Plantain Lilies. "And the succulents were brought from Arizona. I got the caladiums and the Boston fern from a nursery in town."

"Your roommate went with you, didn't he? The one who likes you?"

"Corey doesn't *like* me."

Victor smothered a bout of laughter against Michael's neck. "He watches you," he whispered, teeth teasing the hollow of his throat. "He notices when your shirt rides up." A single claw dragged between his ribs. "When you straighten your back and square your shoulders." Lips parted over his skin. "He's conscious of every move you make."

Michael couldn't deny the way his body heated, how he bared his neck and savored Victor's playful possessiveness. "You jealous?"

"I saw you first," he teased.

"You hunted me like I was prey."

"Does that bother you?"

*No.* It didn't bother Michael and that was the problem. He enjoyed the way Victor reacted to him, how he caged him against counters and walls, the rasp in his voice when he told him what to do and how to do it, how he took enough from Michael to surprise him, but never took anything that wasn't being offered.

"I'd tell you if it did," Michael said. He closed his eyes and placed his hands over Victor's, following each touch. A warm palm drifted down his side, the other smoothed over the top of his jeans and slid between his thighs. He bit his bottom lip. "Janice is on her way home. Like, right now. She could be here any..." A gasp cut his sentence in half. He pushed on Victor's knuckles, guiding him. *There.* His hips twitched and he closed his eyes. "Any minute."

"You're right, we should stop." Victor mapped the freckles on his neck with featherlight passes of his lips. He thumbed at Michael's nipple and rubbed him through his jeans, teasing and taunting until Michael's mouth quivered and his body trembled and—

"Jesus fucking Christ," Michael hissed.

Victor chuckled against the shell of his ear. "Interesting choice of words."

Michael gripped Victor's hand where it was settled over his chest. He almost unbuttoned his jeans, almost grabbed Victor's wrist and demanded to be touched. But a car door closed. Victor hummed knowingly against his cheek. The front door opened. "What a shame," Victor purred. He pressed a quick kiss to Michael's racing pulse. "Have fun at dinner." Then he disappeared, leaving Michael to catch himself on the edge of the door, flushed and breathless and alone on the balcony.

"You're kidding." The ghost of Victor's hands left his body aching. Michael stomped inside and glared at the ceiling. *"Seriously?"*

No one answered. The attic door didn't open. A demon didn't step from the shadows.

"Hey! Anyone home?" Janice called. "Oh, hi, Corey. Seen my brother?" Her keys jingled. Heeled boots made hooved sounds on the wood floors. "Michael, you ready? I'm starving!"

"Thanks." Sarcasm coated his voice, eyes still pinned to the ceiling. "You're *such* an asshole." He shrugged on his coat, adjusted his jeans and combed his fingers through his hair. *Okay. Dinner.* There was no getting rid of the blush burning high in his cheeks. "Hey, yeah!" He cleared his throat and grabbed the ratty shoes seated next to his bedroom door, tugging them on as he stumbled down the hall. *Food. Sister. Concentrate.* "I'm..." He snorted and rolled his eyes. "I'm coming, sorry!"

JANICE INSISTED ON going to one of the breweries downtown. They sat at a small, round high top in the crowded pub, sipping fancy red ales over a pretzel appetizer.

"They make this cheese-mustard-whatever dip with the house IPA. It's good, huh?" Janice tore a piece off the pretzel and dipped it in the hot, yellow sauce. Her vibrant hair was beginning to fade on the ends, turning pink where it should've been red.

Michael nodded and followed her lead, ripping, dipping and taking a bite. "It's pretty awesome. Good call."

"I told you!" She slapped crumbs off her palms. "People love this place. It's a local hangout, I guess."

"That diner Corey took me to was pretty good too. The one right across from Crescent Café?"

"Yeah, how'd that go by the way?" Janice's smile thinned. She lifted her eyebrows and averted her gaze to the table. Michael knew that expression. He'd seen it countless times over the course of his life. Seeing it attached to Corey made him sit back in his chair and scoff. "Don't do that," she warned, laughing through it. "I know you, Michael. You're my little brother, I know when you're screwing around, and I can tell—"

"You think I'm fucking Corey?"

The couple at the table next to them glanced away from their plates. Janice hushed him.

Michael's top lip curled. He scooted closer and lowered his voice. "You think I'm sleeping with our roommate? For real, Jan? You think I'm that fucking *dumb?*"

"Yes," she blurted, and it sounded like *obviously*. "I don't think you're that dumb, you *are* that dumb. Remember Christian?"

"Doesn't count."

"Andy?"

"Circumstantial."

"He was my boyfriend!" Janice exclaimed. Laughter sliced through her words like a knife.

Michael sipped his beer. "I was drunk, it was four years ago, and it was once."

It wasn't once.

"Michael, honestly." Janice's hazel eyes rolled toward the ceiling where old beer bottles were strung together, dipping low over each table like lanterns. Different colored bulbs glowed inside them. "We've been here for less than a week and you're already..." She flicked her wrist at him. "Doing what you always do."

"And what do I always do?"

"Dive into the first pair of pretty eyes that pays any attention to you," Janice said. She rested her mouth against the rim of her glass. "For real, though. Corey's cute. He's really cute—way cuter than he sounded on the phone. But he's our roommate and I don't wanna have to explain to our landlord how Corey moved out on a whim because my brother kicked his heart in the ass, okay?"

"I'm not hooking up with Corey. We went to breakfast, he gave me a ride to the nursery so I could pick up some plants, that's it. He's..." Michael ran his palm over his chin and mouth. "We flirt a little bit, I guess. But it's nothing. It's really, *really* nothing."

She leaned over the table, eyes narrowed like they always were when she'd sniffed him out. Whether it was fresh cuts under his clothes or finding out he'd been sleeping with the neighbor's husband or hearing gossip about another heart he'd left in the gutter, somehow, Janice always uncovered Michael's secrets. "Well, you haven't picked up your books for class, you've been"—she curled her fingers into air quotations—"*chillin' at home* for the last three days, and I literally found an empty bottle of lube in the trash, so who are you having sex with?"

This one, however, was an unusually packaged secret.

Michael flashed a sarcastic, toothy smile. "It could've been Corey's lube."

"It was vanilla flavored."

"And?"

"*Michael*," Janice seethed.

"Nobody," Michael said.

"Bullshit."

"I'm serious!"

"You're seriously lying," she mocked.

Michael heaved a frustrated sigh. He took another long sip off his beer and shook his head. If she wanted to know, he'd tell her. "Fine. I am seeing someone! How's that? I'm seeing someone and"—he slammed his glass down—"we've been having mind-blowing sex"—propped his elbow on the table—"all over our haunted ass house"—and promptly extended his middle finger—"that we rented in this creepy ass town."

Janice rolled her eyes again. "Fuck you too. Who?"

"The poltergeist, that's who," he snapped.

"Oh, right, the poltergeist." Janice snorted a laugh. God, she sounded exactly like their mom. "Look, whoever it is, just make sure it isn't Corey, okay? He's off limits."

"Sure, fine, Corey has officially been placed on the do-not-screw list. Happy?"

Janice shrugged and lifted her menu. "I'd be happier if you actually intended on going to class next week."

"You planned this, didn't you?" Michael rested his chin on the heel of his palm and watched her, eyebrows raised, smile forged and horrible. "You said you wanted to hang out with me because you've been *so* busy. But really, you wanted to do this, huh? Trap me."

"Is trying to have an honest conversation with you trapping you?"

"You sound just like Mom."

"She wasn't wrong about everything. You should go to school," she said, voice softening as she reached over to clutch his hand. She passed her thumb over an old, jagged scar on his wrist. "Your classes are paid for, all you have to worry about are books and supplies. You can pick whatever major you want—hell, you could take philosophy if you wanted! Or astrology! Or horticulture!" She grinned over the last word and squeezed his hand. "A couple writing courses wouldn't hurt your blogging platform either."

"It's not really a platform." Michael's mood perked at the mention of the only thing he had that was exclusively his. Something the Gates name wasn't attached to. "Travel agencies and hostels ask me to write about my experiences abroad. That's it."

"You forgot the paying you part," Janice said matter-of-factly and snatched the last piece of the pretzel.

"Lots of bloggers get paid."

"No, *some* bloggers get paid. You make enough money to get by, which is saying something."

He couldn't argue with that. "Mom and Dad would absolutely lose their minds if they found out I majored in Horticulture with a minor in Journalism."

Janice's grin turned wicked and playful, a reminder that even when they fought and hissed and hurt each other, they were still the Gates siblings; even if he successfully chased everyone else away, she would still be there with a beer and a lecture.

"Then don't tell them," she whispered.

Michael's lips split into a wolfish grin. When she lifted her beer, he lifted his, and she tapped their glasses together.

"See?" Her brows arched. "Problem solved."

A server stopped by to see if they needed anything. Janice offered to pay for the next round, IPAs this time, and they both ordered entrees. The conversation was lighter after that. Janice teased him about Corey. They laughed and reminisced over stories from back home—the night Janice had stolen their dad's truck, Michael waking up in the valedictorian's bed after junior prom, the theater parties they'd crashed and people they'd dated and memories they kept close. Their old life seeped into this one, and soon they both had their elbows on the table, leaning close to whisper about the local college and how Port Lewis seemed more alive than Phoenix. Janice swore it was the forest. *More oxygen*, she assured him. *Less pollutants*. But Michael knew what made Port Lewis feel watched and alive, like its heartbeat was buried deep beneath concrete and tangled in ancient roots. *Magic*, he thought. But he didn't say a word. They cycled through subjects. First it was their parents, then it was the grocery list, and then Michael hinted at Janice's nonexistent love life.

"Hey, now," she shot back, suppressing a laugh. "I'm freshly single, thank you very much."

They laughed together like they always did and stole bites off each other's food like they always did. Finally, Michael got to the truth and she told him about the guy in her Anthropology class who had bought her coffee last week.

"He wears these cute reading glasses and he's, like, I don't know, he's just sweet," Janice said. Her cheeks turned pink and she smiled sheepishly at the burger on her plate. "I'm gonna play it cool and invite him to the party this weekend."

"Good plan," Michael said.

He didn't tell her anything about the demon who lived in their attic.

It was strange keeping a secret as uncharted and mystical as Victor was. And even if Michael told her the truth, even if he found a way to put his feelings for Victor into words and laid them out, raw and honest and awful, Janice still wouldn't believe him. Not really. Not completely.

And not because of what Victor happened to be, but because of what Michael had always been.

Incapable of anything long-term. Allergic to affection. The definition of *commitment issues.*

"Mom wanted me to ask about you." Janice chewed on the inside of her cheek and shot him a wilted smile. "Like, *about* you."

"She wanted you to check for cat scratches, right?" Michael steered his eyes to the window lit by glowing beer signs, streaked with tiny drops of rain.

Janice let out a slow breath. "Yeah, I guess. She wanted me to ask if you were self-medicating again."

"Self-medicating?" Michael's brows shot up.

"That's what her therapist calls it."

"Of course it is," he said under his breath. The scars on his arms and hips and thighs buzzed beneath the ink he'd hidden them with. Even if they were covered by his clothes—the line on his collarbone and the two deeper marks on his ribs—they felt seen, somehow. "I'm not sad, Jan. I never... She doesn't have to worry. No one needs to worry that I'll..." He finished the rest of his beer, buying time to think of the right way to say what he needed to say. "Sometimes I need to *feel* it, you know?"

"Feel what?"

"Alive."

"Do you need to feel that way to *stay* alive?"

"No," he snapped. His lips pressed into a line and he shifted his jaw from side to side. "I'm fine, okay? It's hard to explain and I wish I had a way to convince you, but I don't. All I've got is the same promise I've made over and over."

"The same promise you've broken."

"Don't do that," Michael warned. He bristled, shoulders pulled tight, back rigid in his seat. "I've always promised I'd come to you if I needed to. I've never promised to stop cutting."

There it was. Janice flinched at the sound of it, tinny in his mouth, an off-limits word whispered between family members and tossed away like dirty laundry. *Cutting.* Something that needed cleaning. Something unfit for a person who wore the last name Gates.

Michael sighed through his nose. "I don't expect you to understand, but I do expect you to trust me."

"Is it..." Janice exhaled, as if she'd been holding onto something and suddenly couldn't anymore. She squeezed her eyes shut. "Is it a sexual thing?"

Michael blinked. His sister's expression was almost desperate, pained and hopeful, and a little embarrassed. "Sometimes," he said, and it was the truth. "Usually it's a control thing."

"Not a depression thing?"

"No, not always."

"But it can be?"

"It hasn't been for a long, long time."

"You promise?"

"*Yes*," he said through another deep sigh. "I promise, Janice."

Really, it was a power thing. Michael had always been soft—his body, his eyes, his voice—and he wanted people to see him as more than that. The last time he'd dragged a blade across his skin, he'd been in the bathroom prepping for a night with the man next door. When Christian had been inside him, bending him over a dresser next to a framed photo from his wedding day, Michael had dug his fingernails into the fresh cuts on his hip until pain unfurled alongside pleasure.

He remembered Christian's shock at the sight of blood.

He remembered the way *twink* rolled off his tongue like a curse. How he'd said *you're a toy, sweetheart* when Michael asked about his wife.

But that shock was a weapon. How his eyes went wide. The way he paused and met Michael's gaze, suddenly, effortlessly plucked from his place of power. That was the real reason.

Michael got off on knocking kings from their thrones, especially when they didn't belong there.

"Was that weird?" Janice whined. "I mean, you don't think it's weird, right? We've always talked about sex together, but if that's like, something you don't wanna—"

"It's only weird if you make it weird," Michael sang.

"Right, yeah, okay." She cleared her throat, lifted her chin to catch their server's attention, and politely said, "Can we get the check, please?"


FOXGLOVE LANE WAS a short street. Four houses lined each side, all Victorian, eclectic and sleepy, with cars in the driveways, fences around lawns, and mailboxes posted on the sidewalk. Darkness draped the neighborhood in sameness. The houses all cast shadows that stretched toward the asphalt and some wore glowing windows that flickered like restless eyes. But only one of the eight appeared to be haunted.

The Lewellyn house, with its gray shingles and blotchy paint, rickety porch and not quite empty attic, looked the part. *Witches lived here*, it said. *I am alive.*

Janice pulled the keys from the ignition. A tree-shaped air freshener dangled from the rearview mirror and textbooks cluttered the backseat of her old Volvo. "Tonight was a trap, you were right about that," she said softly, admittance light and whispered. She nodded to herself and her lips thinned into a forced smile. "But I love you, Michael. I *do*. I want to go to dinner with you just to go, and hang out just to hang out, and not have to…"

*Try*. The word was right there. Even though she didn't let it slip, it hurt all the same.

"I understand," Michael said. He did and he didn't. Time had shaped them into different people. "Don't worry about it."

Janice who was ambitious and loving and sweet, and Michael who was none of those things in the same way she was, had grown apart in ways most siblings did. Janice didn't understand the things about Michael that he barely understood himself. And Michael couldn't fathom living the life Janice was desperate to live. Something safe. Something predictable.

"I love you too," Michael added.

Her smile widened. She didn't say anything else about their conversation at the pub, but she did lean over the center console and press a kiss to his cheek. The car beeped when she locked it and the porch squeaked under their shoes. Sadness or something close to sadness bloomed in his chest. He'd worried her for a long time, he thought. Despite being attached at the hip through high school, going to the same parties, sharing the same friend group—*still*—she held onto the one night he'd gone a little too deep, the one time there had been a little too much blood, the one weak moment that wouldn't go away.

*I was sixteen.* Michael thumbed at the cigarette pack in his coat pocket. *I was a mess.*

"Do you smell that?" Janice tilted her chin back and sniffed. "Cookies?"

"Brownies," he said.

"Weird. I didn't take Corey for a baker. Think he left us some?"

"Eh, I dunno, but I'm going to bed anyway. See you tomorrow."

"It's eight o'clock," Janice teased.

Michael snorted. He hollered a sarcastic *goodnight* to her from the top of the stairs and locked his bedroom door behind him. It was hard to focus with memories clawing at the edge of his vision. Blood on white tiles. Fear. Red smeared over his phone when he opened Janice's message bubble and typed: *I need help.*

The pleasant smell of chocolate filled his bedroom. Victor stood in the doorway that led to the balcony, shoulder propped against the frame, gazing into the night. He didn't stir at Michael's footsteps, didn't make a sound when Michael plucked a brownie from the plate on his nightstand. Stillness looked uneasy on him, especially with his back turned and his attention elsewhere.

"Do you miss it?" Michael asked. He trailed his fingers along the edge of the white door and stepped onto the balcony, following Victor's gaze to the sky.

A soft, dismissive breath fogged the air in front of Victor's mouth. "Sometimes."

Michael glanced at him, at his fiercely handsome face and long neck, down to where his shirt slouched too far, exposing just enough of his clavicle to display a hickey Michael had left last night. He remembered Victor's fingers on his own collarbones, trailing a scar, on his hip, on his wrist—

"What's wrong?" Victor took Michael's jaw in a loose grip. "Are they not good?"

"What?"

"The brownies."

"Oh, no, I haven't..." Michael huffed a laugh and brought the brownie to his mouth. It was rich, soft in the middle and laced with caramel ribbons. Victor passed his thumb over the corner of his lips. "Holy shit," he slurred, chewing and swallowing before he continued. "You can bake? Like, *really* bake. What's in these?"

"Cardamom, caramel, maple, and cocoa. They're gluten free."

Michael laughed. *Hard.* Hard enough that he almost choked. "Oh, they're gluten free? Are they low-carb too? Vegan?"

"Flourless." Victor flashed a grin. He pulled a corner off the brownie and popped it in his mouth. "Has no one ever cooked for you before?"

"No," Michael said, reeling in lingering chuckles. The sheer idea of his past partners—if he could even call them that—cooking for him? He barked another laugh. "*Hell no*. Where'd you learn to make these?"

"I was a pastry chef," he said.

Michael paused, the last bite hovering in front of his lips. "What?"

"You heard me."

"You're serious?"

"Dead serious. I used to bake for Crescent Café all the time." He tilted his head, patient and soft, lit by dim moonlight. "Is that surprising?"

He sucked chocolate off his fingers, chewing slowly. "Well, you're..." He gestured to Victor with a flick of his wrist.

"And if I was this?" Victor stepped backward into the bedroom. Light from the lamp on the nightstand poured over him. His edges softened and bent. Magic swept over him and across him, and he was human again. Bright eyes, brown where they'd been gold, and dark hair, longer and undisturbed by the curve of horns, shimmered like a hologram. His smile waned and he dropped his gaze to the floor, thumbs shoved through his belt loops. "Would that make it more believable?"

Michael inhaled sharply through his nose. Guilt knotted uncomfortably in his chest. "I'm..." He followed Victor into the bedroom, watching him take another step back, another, until the glamour was gone, revealing horns and claws. "I didn't mean it like that, I'm sorry. I'm just... I'm not very good at this." He chewed on his bottom lip, cheeks flushed, brownie still sweet on his tongue and between his teeth. "If you haven't noticed."

"I've noticed." Victor sat on the edge of the bed, shoulders loose and bare feet light on the floor.

Michael's heart kicked. He bit down harder on his lip and fidgeted, picking uselessly at his nail beds. Victor was in front of him. Awful memories flashed behind his eyes. Janice's voice replayed over and over, the moment she'd stopped before she could say *try*.

*Try to love you. Try to like you. Try to understand you.*

"I hit a vein when I was sixteen," he blurted.

Victor lifted his face and watched him, waiting.

"I just... It was a fucking accident. My boyfriend at the time walked in on me with someone else and he called me every name in the book, and I—I deserved it, I know that, but I was pissed and upset, and I wanted to feel something else. Just for a second, you know? So, I went a little too deep, and..." He rubbed the scar on his wrist, the one that bled too much, the one that needed stitches. The same one Janice squeezed hours ago. The one Victor kissed days ago. "They called me high risk, like I cut myself for sport or something."

"Well, did you?"

"No," Michael hissed. His eyes narrowed and he dug his fingernails into his wrist. "I didn't... I don't cut because I'm sad, I cut because it gives me power over my pain. It's mine to determine. Mine to harness. Mine to direct. I know that doesn't make sense—"

"It does," Victor said. He tilted his head, eyes trailing Michael's long strides as he paced back and forth across the room. "I get it."

"And then I turned eighteen and started getting tattoos to cover some of the scars. It's the same thing, but people don't question it. They see a sparrow or a skull or words in ink and they think I'm addicted to the pain, to the rush, and maybe I am a little bit." He was rambling. Horribly, messily rambling. "But when I bleed..." He slowed down, easing each word out on individual breaths. "I know no matter where I am or who I'm with or what I'm doing, I control that."

"What about the other night?" Victor asked. He scooted back on the bed until he was propped against the black frame and took another brownie from the plate.

Michael immediately covered the mark on his hip, the place Victor's claw had torn his skin. His sweater was ripped there, exposing the rigid edge of the scab. The house was silent. He listened for footsteps or the TV or music, but there was nothing. Janice was probably reading. Corey was working a night shift at the theater. He held his breath, watching Victor's candlewick eyes glint in the low light.

The answer burned in his throat. He rolled the hem of his sweater between his fingers and pulled it over his head. Victor stopped chewing. "You're talking about this, right?" Michael knew exactly what Victor was talking about, but he slipped his palm over his hip and pushed his jeans down to show the wound in its entirety, framed by two, pale fingers.

Victor tilted his head back. His nostrils flared. He swept his gaze over Michael's torso. "Yeah, I'm talking about that," he said, failing to conceal the darkness in his voice, as if a thousand other people had whispered when he spoke.

Michael set his hands on the bed. He crawled over Victor's legs, thighs on either side of his hips, and eased over his lap. They were incredibly close. Victor's breath played on Michael's chin, his free hand curled around the back of Michael's thigh. Like this, on his knees, he looked down at Victor, into unrelenting golden eyes, mouth close to the curve of his right horn.

"You cut me open because you lost control," Michael rasped. He took Victor's hand, covered in crumbs and chocolate and caramel, and brought it to his mouth. "And you lost control because of me." He dragged his lips over Victor's fingers, opened his mouth and sucked sweetness off his claws. Victor's breath stuttered. He gripped Michael's thigh harder, eyelids heavy, tongue darting out to wet his lips. "Or did I misread the situation?"

Victor hummed, a deep, low sound that crackled and sparked.

Michael touched Victor's knuckles, dragged his fingers to the place where his thumb jutted from his palm. He let his weight press into the warm body beneath him, grinding down enough to make Victor's breath catch again, to make his hips jerk and his claws sink in. He let go of Victor's hand and touched the sigil on his chest.

"I know I'm fucked up," Michael whispered. "But I've never been with anyone who made letting go and not being in control feel—" *safe* "—easy. I figured you should know that."

"You haven't let go yet." Victor's mouth dusted his jaw.

He closed his eyes, enduring the painfully slow glide of Victor's hand down his chest, over his belly, to his jeans. Michael's breath left him, returning in the form of a sharp gasp. He framed Victor's neck, thumbs poised at the hinges of his jaw, and said, "You make me want to."

Victor tilted his head until their lips touched. They tasted like sugar and cardamom. Michael closed his eyes and kissed him back, quietly, slowly. He let Victor set the pace, allowed himself to be soft, to be held and grabbed and touched. He felt small in Victor's arms, and for once it did not make him feel less powerful. Somehow, being with Victor didn't make him feel less of anything.

"You're not fucked up," Victor said. His arms were tight around him, claws tickling the space where Michael's shoulder blades shadowed his skin. Dark, long lashes swept up and down, from Michael's mouth to his eyes. "But we do make quite a pair, me and you."

"But you're just a pastry chef," Michael teased under his breath.

Victor's smile was loose and playful. "And you're just a gardener."

The very tips of Michael's fingers disappeared into Victor's short hair. An honest laugh—the kind that came after apprehension, the kind that came before happiness—filled the space between their lips. He tugged

Victor into another kiss. This one lingered. It grew and stretched and deepened until Michael's lungs ached and his cheeks flushed, until his hips stirred and his back arched. Victor pulled his bottom lip between his teeth. Something vicious lived in his voice, even here, like this, panting and undone and impossibly gentle. He said Michael's name and whispers crawled over each syllable.

"What do you want?" Victor asked.

Michael wanted Victor's teeth in his neck. He wanted blood to pool under Victor's claws. He wanted Victor on his knees. On top of him, underneath him, anywhere, *everywhere.*

But more than anything, Michael wanted something he'd been too stubborn to give, and too afraid to accept. Tenderness, maybe. Trust, definitely.

"Tell me," Victor said. He pressed his lips to Michael's neck, his shoulder. Warm hands palmed his ass, pulling him into a slow, sensuous grind.

"Just..." He didn't know how to ask for what he wanted. Instead, he fumbled between them, hurriedly unbuttoning their jeans, then took Victor's hand, parted his lips over the deep line curving from his wrist to his middle finger, and licked his palm.

There was too much to say. Michael Gates had arrived in Port Lewis a week ago, hoping for change, for newness and growth and recognition. He wanted to find himself, maybe. Or he wanted to find the pieces most people claimed he'd buried under scars and ink and cruelty. But he'd landed here instead, rolling his hips in Victor's lap with his jeans pushed to his thighs, fucking into the clawed fingers wrapped around his cock, trembling and *close* and slow.

Victor kissed him again, tongue hot and familiar behind his teeth. When he pulled back, he lingered, lips slippery on his chin. "Can I put my mouth on you?"

Michael nodded. He hadn't expected to be pressed into the bed, chest down, with Victor's lips at the base of his spine. But he didn't tell him to stop, not when his teeth nipped Michael's thigh, not when there was breath between his legs and Victor's tongue pressing inside him. He dug his fingers into the sheets and muffled a whine, burying his face in the bed. Heat unspooled wherever Victor touched. He opened his mouth wide, tongue stroking and curling, pushing in deep and licking across his perineum. Each movement brought Michael closer.

Victor kept him there, teetering on the edge, whimpering and gasping and weak. *Please.* He wouldn't beg, he wouldn't. His hips jerked and his breath caught.

Finally, Victor eased away. He turned Michael onto his back, tugging his jeans until they were gone, and pressed two fingers against his hole. Glamour was a strange thing. He knew claws *should* be there. He anticipated them, sharp and curved, but they were gone. Fuck, magic was amazing, how the hell did he ever live without it? Michael hadn't grabbed the lube from his nightstand, and still, Victor's fingers were hot and wet.

"Can you come like this?" Victor's voice sounded as wrecked as Michael felt. He held Michael down with a hand on his belly, the other busy between his legs, fingers sliding in as deep as they could, rubbing hard and perfect against his prostate.

Michael's mouth trembled. His cock ached, dark and leaking below his belly button. "If you tell me to," he whispered.

Victor's bottom lip paled under the weight of his teeth. He watched Michael, flushed and focused, eyes alight in the barely lit room. He slid his palm from Michael's belly to his chest, claw passing over his nipple before he settled his thumb and index finger low on his throat. He didn't squeeze or grip. Michael's airway stayed unobstructed, but the idea that Victor could choke him—that Michael wanted him to—made pleasure twist in his stomach and heat throb between his thighs.

Victor leaned over him, arm flexed, fingers curled deep inside him, wrist pumping again and again. Michael met his gaze, eyelashes fluttering, jaw slack and breath shallow. He waited, watching Victor's lips part, enduring fast, hard, relentless strokes, before Victor said, "I want to see you lose control." He tipped his face closer. Fingers pressed in and twisted. "I want to watch you come for me."

A car rolled into the driveway. The front door opened and Corey's voice cut through the quiet house. *Hey, Janice.* Michael kept his eyes on Victor.

"You're so fucking beautiful," Victor hissed. His fingers pressed against Michael's prostate again, circling and rubbing, and Michael's body surged.

Jaw slack, eyes fixed on Victor, Michael came on a silent, breathless cry. He clawed at the bed, hips jumping and quivering. Everything within him tightened—his abdomen, his chest, the muscles in his legs. Staying quiet was difficult. His eyelashes were wet, pleasure thrashed inside him, come splattered his stomach, and all he wanted to do was gasp and whine. But he swallowed every whimper, choked back the shout threatening in his throat, and turned to bite the sheets instead.

The kitchen sink ran. Michael didn't bother trying to catch his breath. Janice's voice was distant, traveling from the living room. *How was work?*

He pushed Victor's pants out of the way and wrapped his fingers around his cock. Victor was poised above him on his hands and knees, breathing fast, teeth still deep in his bottom lip.

*Where's Michael?*

He circled his thumb over the head of Victor's cock, satisfied when a breath punched out of him.

*I guess he's in bed already.*

Eye contact was different like this, with Victor's heavy cock in his hand, feeling him pulse and twitch, brows knitted, eyes blazing—completely, utterly under Michael's spell. Victor gasped, grinding down between his spread legs, coming hot and sudden over his fingers and hip. He kissed Michael hard to smother a moan, the sound low and primal in his mouth.

The bedroom was unusually quiet.

Laughter and conversation disrupted the first floor.

Michael listened to footsteps on the stairs. He closed his eyes and touched Victor's waist, stillness unspooling between them as their breathing slowed and their bodies sank into the bed. This secret burned in him. He dusted his fingers over Victor's ribs, his shoulders, then lightly curled his hands around black horns. They kissed again, careless and slow, passing breath and nipping lips and licking slowly into each other's mouths.

A door in the hall opened and closed. Corey's, probably. The floorboards squeaked. His chest lurched when he felt the intense intimacy of their bodies sliding together, torso to torso. Their quivering limbs. Their swollen lips. The remnants of what they'd done to each other still wet and warm on their skin.

*So this is what it feels like.* Michael went boneless beneath him. A smile tugged at his lips as Victor pressed kiss after kiss to his cheek, his jaw, the corner of his mouth. Some people called it aftercare. Others assumed aftercare was too big a word to pair with sex as tender as they'd just had. But Michael thought the definition was flexible. Being praised with touch and steadiness was more important to him after sex that felt like making love than it did with sex that left him sore and bleeding.

Satisfaction came in different shapes and sizes, and this particular satisfaction bloomed in comfortable numbness. His body buzzed, still chasing remnants of a white-hot orgasm. Victor mapped the freckles on his shoulders with his lips.

"Is this okay?" Victor asked. He pressed his cheek to Michael's collarbone and let out a long breath.

Michael's hands slipped from his horns and landed on the bed above his head. "For a minute, yeah. But I want a cigarette."

A clawed finger guided Michael's chin to the side. Victor looked at him, his features cut into gorgeous lines. "Don't ever be ashamed to ask me for something. If you wanna bleed, I'll make you bleed. If you want me to be gentle, I'll be gentle."

Heat blistered in Michael's cheeks. He swallowed hard and nodded.

Victor held his gaze. "But blood magic... It's complicated. You're human, and I don't know what'll happen if I handle your blood in a situation where I'm..." He paused, lips parted as he searched for the word. "Compromised."

"What's complicated about it?"

"Everything."

Michael snorted. "Are you always this vague?"

"It's what killed me," Victor said.

The air tilted again. That same, ancient wrongness returned, acrid and sharp on Michael's tongue. Lights flickered. Corey's voice came from his bedroom across the hall. *Whoa, power's acting weird.* Victor rolled away and grabbed his shirt from the floor, wiping his stomach with it before he handed it to Michael.

He wished he could hit rewind again. Go back to ten seconds ago, sprawled on the bed post-orgasm with a handsome demon draped over his chest. But curiosity gnawed on him. *The last person I slept with is the same person who killed me.* Victor's words echoed from a memory, clouded with steam, a prelude to the beginning of them, whatever they were. *It's what killed me.* Night split apart and unearthed their uncomfortable truths. His and Victor's.

Michael found sweats on the floor. Victor tugged his jeans back on. It was too cold to stand on the balcony, so Michael cracked the door and leaned against it, cigarette balanced between his lips. He waited, inhaling deeply when Victor's breath ignited the paper. Smoke filled his lungs, coaxed his shoulders to droop and his head to loll, resting on the edge of the door.

Tobacco always tasted better after good sex. He eyed Victor carefully, smoke stinging in his throat, then closed the space between them and exhaled into Victor's mouth, passing breath and smoke and a whisper. "Will you tell me what happened?"

Another exhale. Another inhale. Another kiss stitched with smoke.

"I was sleeping with a necromancer," Victor said. He crossed his arms over his chest and turned to look at the sky, dotted with stars and lit by a smiling moon. "They were young, well, not *young*. Your age, maybe. It was fun and fast and dangerous, and completely fucking forbidden." That was not an unfamiliar word to him—*forbidden*. It came out abused, as if he'd said it over and over again, slathered with sarcasm and attached to things Michael didn't know. "We pushed too far. I knew it. They knew it. We just... We didn't stop when we should've. They saw where I was taking magic and I trusted Vassa enough to let them go there with me."

Quietly, Michael said, "Go where with you?"

Victor took the cigarette from between Michael's fingers. "I told them about Allocer, how I'd contacted him, what I intended to do, and they didn't tell the elders. They didn't tell my mom, didn't tell Margo, they didn't even tell Jordan." He snorted over Jordan's name, another person Michael didn't know, but he nodded anyway and listened. "The deal I made with Allocer"—he tapped a single, long claw over the scar on his chest—"is that death seals my soul to his energy. We integrate—become one being, one entity—where his magic and my magic are both free to flow through this body. As long as my soul is alive, corporeal, and my memories are intact, he has a strong, living vessel to merge with, and I have power and vitality."

"But?"

The paper on the end of the cigarette crackled. "But," Victor said, exhaling gray plumes into the air. "I got cocky. Vassa did too. One night, we were messing around, playing with blood magic. I was letting them syphon from me..." He shifted his gaze to Michael. "Which means they drank my blood and drained my energy. It's alchemy, a kind of magic necromancers use, something you're born with. Anyway, dark magic feels like being high, like... Like, doing ecstasy or coke. And what we were doing was as dark as it gets. They were ripping magic out of me by force, reconstructing it and giving it back in different ways, and we were..." He shrugged. "In bed, distracted. They carved elemental runes onto my collarbone, syphoned until I was tapped out, then..." Victor flicked the cigarette over the edge of the balcony. "Vassa stopped my heart."

Michael wanted to light another cigarette, but he didn't move or breathe or blink.

"It was an accident. A fucked-up accident, yeah, but an accident. Once I died, the contract was sealed. Vassa tried to bring me back, but it was too late. Allocer got there first. I woke up in a pool of my own blood, too out of it to understand what happened. Vassa was standing in the doorway—they looked so scared," he whispered. His brows knitted, jaw slack and eyes far away. "And that was it. Done deal. I'd sealed myself to Allocer in this house, spilled my blood on these floors. It means I'm trapped here until someone uses my blood and Allocer's sigil to call for me. Not that anyone would ever have both those *magical relics* handy," he said, playfulness turning sour as he spoke. "But that's what happened. Now you know."

Terms swirled uncomfortably inside him. *Necromancer. Rune. Trapped. Elemental. Syphon.* He didn't know where to start, what to ask, if he should even attempt to ask. But he would never understand if he didn't try. "Necromancers bring people back from the dead?"

"They can. Necromancers manipulate energy. They can take life, change it, and give it back to the original host or place it somewhere else. Same with magic."

"That's what syphoning is?" Michael tested.

Victor nodded. "You catch on quick."

"And all of this has to do with blood?"

"All of it *starts* with blood. Witches use blood magic—dark magic—to manipulate energy, to feel each other's magic and power. Elemental magic happens here." Victor dragged his knuckle over Michael's arm. "Dark magic happens in here." He tapped on Michael's sternum. "Does that make sense?"

"Not really, but I get it."

"Vassa syphoned to the point where they undid my organs. Another few minutes and my ribs probably would've snapped."

Michael flinched. "That can happen?"

"Yes." Victor leaned closer, breath light and ashy on his mouth. "But it didn't."

"And if I bleed when we're—" he met Victor's eyes and lifted a brow "—or if you… If you taste my blood…" His cheeks burned at the thought. "You think something could happen to me?"

He tipped his head, lips gentle as they pressed against Michael's. "Not unless I can syphon from you, and honestly? I don't know if I can. But I'll feel you, all of you. I'll see things; I'll know what you're experiencing."

"And if I taste your blood?"

"You'll feel all of me too."

"Do witches and necromancers and whatever the hell *isn't* human in this town usually date humans?"

Victor's lips split into a grin. He curled his fingers around Michael's hip and smoothed his palm over his ass to the top of his thigh. "Are you implying we're dating?"

Yes, that's exactly what he was implying. "No," he bit out, eyes narrowed and mouth pinched. "Of course not."

"C'mon."

Michael scoffed.

Victor's grin widened. "You're charming. Do you know that? Do people tell you that?"

"Fuck you."

He kissed the corner of Michael's frown, his cheek, his jaw. "Most of us rarely date humans, but it happens."

"And if anyone at Hogwarts knew we were doing this?"

Laughter sputtered out of Victor. "They'd tell me to wipe your memory and send you on your way."

Another kiss to Michael's chin. Another held breath and strange truth and heavy consequence.

"What if I wanted to remember you?" Michael closed his eyes, defeated, and tipped forward to tuck his face into Victor's neck. An owl hooted in the distance and the night sang to them in varying tones—rustling bushes, claws on tree bark, a neighborhood cat meowing as it crossed a fence. Michael wasn't good at this, at liking someone, at having feelings and urges and desires that weren't paired with an escape plan. Victor set his chin on the top of Michael's head, their bodies pressed close, swaying back and forth in the silent, sleepy house. When Victor didn't answer, Michael sighed against his copper skin. "Do you really think I'm charming?"

Victor's chest rumbled, a short, lovely chuckle. "I think you're insufferable and smart and prideful, but yeah, I think you're charming too."

"I'm sorry about what happened to you."

"I'm sorry you feel the need to be sorry," Victor replied. He pushed the French door closed with his foot and nudged Michael toward the bed. "We were warned. *I* was warned. But me and Vassa didn't listen. We made mistakes. I don't regret becoming what I am now, I just wish Vassa hadn't been there to watch it happen."

Michael kicked the dirty sheets to the floor. Victor slipped out of his jeans, crawled in beside him and settled beneath the comforter, warm and solid under Michael's cheek. Claws tickled his back, across his shoulders and down his spine. Chills followed each sharp point on his skin. He closed his eyes, curled over Victor's chest, lulled and satisfied and hungry for more.

More of Victor's story. More of his life. More of his magic.

More of *him*.

"Did you love them?" Michael asked. He straddled the line between asleep and awake.

"Vassa?"

"Yeah."

Victor's hand paused low on his back. "Platonically, I think. We had a physical relationship, but it was never romantic."

"Is that something you're interested in? Romantic stuff?"

"I baked you brownies," Victor said matter-of-factly.

"Friends bake each other brownies. Platonic partners do too."

His voice softened. "Are *you* interested in romantic stuff?"

Michael huffed. "I asked you first."

"I'm not the one with a laundry list of lovers left behind in Arizona."

"They weren't lovers—I mean, a couple of them were, I guess. But I just… I never really tried. I had *one* romantic relationship—maybe, if it even counts—with the boyfriend I cheated on when I was sixteen. Ever since then?" He shook his head. "Just didn't happen."

Victor stayed quiet for a long time. His claws resumed their dance across his back, drawing patterns on his vertebrae and over his ribs. "I'd like to date you, Michael. Romantically."

Michael curled closer to him. No one had ever said it that easily before. Usually he was being courted by a drunk guy at a party, or worse, riding a married man in the bed he shared with a loving, naïve wife. Or on his knees listening to whispered praise—*I'd buy you a collar and call you mine if I could*—wondering if Janice knew her boyfriend was screwing him in the locker room every day after football practice. Michael wasn't a good person. He used people and got used by them, and no one had ever questioned that.

The simple way Victor said it—*I'd like to date you*—shook him to his core.

"Christian used to tell me I was a toy. No batteries required," Michael muttered. He kept his eyes closed and listened to the thrum of Victor's dark heart. "I was still in high school when we started messing around. Just turned eighteen. He was thirty-five."

"Is this the guy who lived next door?"

"Yeah, the one who married the pre-school teacher. I used her perfume whenever I went over there. Even wore her lipstick once."

"Did she ever find out?"

"I don't know," Michael said softly. Victor hadn't stopped touching him and Michael hadn't opened his eyes, and still, everything felt at ease. Even after he'd said Christian's name out loud. Even when he said, "He told me he loved me." Which wasn't exactly the truth. Christian said things like *I love your mouth* and *you're so tight, I love you like this*. And Michael, never, ever believed him. "Why the hell would you want to date someone like me?"

"Someone like you?"

Someone who wouldn't allow themselves to feel anything until it was too late. Someone who was lonely and awful and covered in scars, who cried during orgasm because vulnerability was addictive and terrifying—someone who had a past he could not scrub clean.

Victor pressed his lips to Michael's temple. "Someone adventurous and interesting? Someone too stubborn for their own good, who's brave and smart and funny? The real question is, why would someone like *you* stay in a house like this with a thing like *me?*"

"Rent control," Michael whispered.

Victor swatted him playfully on the hip.

"You're kind and gentle, and apparently you can cook. I'd be an idiot not to pursue this."

"Is that it?"

"I'm sure I'll get used to the horns."

"You love the horns," Victor purred.

A raspy laugh filled the room. "Yeah, I kinda do."

Carefully, Victor turned until they were face to face. He kept his arm curled over Michael's waist, eyes wild and bright in the dark. "I like you, Michael Gates. You seem to think I shouldn't, but I do."

"I like you too." Michael heaved a sigh and set his palm on Victor's cheek. "And I want to date you too. Romantically."

Victor's smile split into a grin. "All right."

"Okay," Michael said. He tilted his head until their noses brushed. Victor craned over him, his sharp frame slicing through the dim moonlight that slipped through the glass-paneled doors. "Okay," he said again, softer this time.

Midnight unraveled around them. Wings beat the air over the balcony. A fire pit crackled from a nearby backyard. Somewhere in the distance, a wolf howled. Michael listened to the night come alive, to Victor breathe, to the bed shift and the house creak, and to their lips meeting again and again.

# Part Five: Oh, Elizabeth

SUNLIGHT POURED ACROSS the bed.

The house held onto the brittle cold from the night before. Morning was still brisk with fog and nearly frozen dew. But Michael woke to warmth on his face. The sun had broken through the cloud cover and lit the paneled French doors and the small balcony, turning his succulents varying shades of yellow and ivy. Port Lewis always wore a grim, gray sky. But like this, cracked open by persistent light, it was beautiful.

Victor Lewellyn was also beautiful. He slept on his back, chest rising and falling with each breath he took. His skin was the color of polished wood, gold in some places, ruddy in others, and speckled black where freckles would've been if he were still human. A few black marks splashed over his right shoulder, barely noticeable. More flecked the back of his hand where the opaque color at his fingertips faded.

Michael brushed his knuckle over the curve of Victor's right horn, following it to his temple, his cheek. They'd gone to bed together, fallen asleep together, but never slept together. Because waking followed sleeping, and Michael had always woken up alone.

Victor's lashes fluttered. Flames licked the whites of his eyes, golden tendrils reflecting the light. "Morning," he rasped.

"Hi." Michael's finger trailed his jaw. He looked at him, really looked. The scars on his collarbone, the sigil on his chest, how he seemed softer this morning, bare and sleepy and beside him. For a moment, he felt caught. As if finding Victor as unbelievably attractive as he did was wrong, somehow. The tendon flexed in his throat should not look as kissable as it did right then. His horns should not look touchable; his body should not be climbable.

But Victor was all those things.

Demon or not, monster or not, pastry chef or not, Michael refused to be embarrassed over wanting him.

Morning turned the sky outside an assortment of Easter blues and sea-stained silver. Night hugged the horizon, a dark stripe that refused to be erased. Frost spiderwebbed the corners of the windows. Michael slid his thighs over Victor's waist, hovering above him. He pulled the comforter over his shoulders to keep the heat in and hummed approvingly as Victor's palms flattened on his lower back.

Their movements were honeyed and slow. Michael rolled his hips, the line of his hard cock prominent through his sweats, and let a soft moan leak over his lips when he felt Victor arch into him, meeting him touch for touch.

"You're insatiable," Victor said, and the way his voice lowered, sexy and encouraging, brought a loose smile to Michael's lips. Claws dipped under the waistband of his sweats. "Take these off."

Michael was flexible, but he wasn't *that* flexible. He almost fell over trying to squirm out of the soft cotton pants. Victor pressed his grin to Michael's shoulder. Michael laughed under his breath until his thighs were around him again, cock grinding against Victor's hip, back arched and mouth open. Victor touched his stomach, dragging his hand over the soft, supple curve of his waist, the line that formed over his sternum in the center of the Atlas moth, the dip between his clavicles. His body was lean, plucked and waxed and carved by scars and ink, smooth and buttery in places some people preferred muscular and solid. But he liked being hairless and grabbable, and seeing the hunger in Victor's eyes coaxed confidence to coil around his bones and squeeze.

"I don't know how you manage to be this gorgeous this *early*," Victor muttered. His thumb found a scar on Michael's ribs, feathered over the moth's wings, and dropped to curl around the base of his cock. "Tell me what you dreamed about."

Michael lifted his hips enough to reach around and guide Victor's cock between his legs. "I—"

A frantic screech echoed from the kitchen. Their quiet morning shattered. Something broke—a coffee mug, probably.

Victor tilted his head, brows knitted and lips quirked. He sat up, curling his arm around Michael's back, and craned to look over his shoulder. "That doesn't sound good."

Michael heaved an annoyed sigh.

Janice's shrill voice cut through the house. "*Spider!*" She kept hollering. A cabinet door slammed. "Holy shit! Michael! Corey! There's a fucking tarantula in the house!"

Victor's breath caught. He looked from the bedroom door to Michael, expression strung somewhere between shock and panic. *Oh no.* "Lizzy," he said, like Michael should know who that was, and a second later he was gone. Tendrils of smoke took his place.

Michael's knees hit the bed. He grabbed the black frame before he fell into it. *God dammit.*

Footsteps smacked the stairs.

"Look!" Janice squealed. "Get it, Corey! Seriously, get it, get it, get it—"

Another horrified scream. A door slammed. Corey shouted, "What the hell was that?"

He almost tripped over his own feet as he stumbled down the stairs, pulling the drawstring tight on his sweats and shoving fingers through his messy hair. Janice stood between the kitchen and the living room in front of the sliding glass door leading to the backyard with a skillet clutched in her hands. Her red hair was tied into a bun atop her head, pajamas askew and sweatshirt slouched over one shoulder.

She jabbed the skillet at the kitchen counter. "A tarantula, Michael? *Seriously?*"

"What?" He inched past the breakfast bar until he saw Corey, standing perfectly still with a thick magazine held above his head, and his adversary, the brown, furry arachnid seated in front of the coffee pot.

"Did you do this to freak us out? To get us to go along with all your poltergeist bullshit?" Janice hissed.

Corey hadn't taken his eyes off the spider, but he said, "Not cool, dude."

"No! Where the hell would I get a tarantula?" Michael glanced from Corey to Janice.

The air stirred. Wind snapped at the windows and rattled the blinds, and suddenly, Victor appeared in the backyard behind Janice, palms flat against the sliding glass door. He met Michael's gaze and hurriedly glanced from him to the spider and back again.

*No.* Michael gave a quick shake of his head. *Hell no.*

"Okay, I'm gonna swat it," Corey said, voice wobbly and unsure.

Victor's eyes widened. He mouthed *please* and curled his fingers, claws scraping the glass. The sound was insignificant, but it was there. A sharp, high-pitched squeak that accompanied very few things. Nails on glass. Rocks on metal. Claws on a window.

Janice whirled around. Corey whipped toward the door. Thankfully, black wisps floated in the air and Victor was gone.

"Fuck, really?" Michael whined under his breath. He wrinkled his nose and trudged into the kitchen. He did not want to handle that spider. It had a thick body and pointed pink toes, and extended its front two legs, waving them defensively as fangs wiggled beneath rows of black eyes. Honestly, he didn't know if he *could* handle it. "We should put it outside," he blurted.

"Yeah, its carcass!" Janice howled.

"What if it's..." Michael stammered, trying to find a way around the situation. "What if it's like, uhm, what— endangered! What if it's endangered or something? We should just catch it and put it in the bushes."

"You're joking," Corey said. He turned to Janice. "He's joking, right?"

When Janice said, "Yes," Michael snapped, "No."

"It could be poisonous!" Corey's blond hair was horribly mussed. His chest heaved, body on a trip wire, arms and stomach and legs flexed for a fight. Michael thought it was a little funny and maybe a little cute that Corey's response to an eight-legged intruder was physical intimidation.

Michael waved his hand at Corey, shooing him. "I'll do it, okay? Just go stand over there with Janice."

Reluctantly, Corey lowered the magazine and did as he was told. Michael swallowed. He kept his eyes glued to the tarantula as he reached into a cabinet for a Tupperware container. The spider jumped, hopping at him with his front legs raised. Michael flew backward and smacked into the breakfast table. Corey yelped. Janice screeched. Even Michael hiccupped on a surprised noise.

"It's fine, I'm fine, I've got it." Michael took slow, small steps. He eased the cabinet open just enough to snatch a container. The spider jumped at him again, a jerky, quick movement that made his heart spike into his throat. "Okay," he whispered, bending his body forward as far as he could, arm outstretched, Tupperware hovering above all eight legs. "Okay, okay..."

"Just do it!" Janice hollered.

Michael dropped the container and clapped both hands over it, holding it firmly to the counter. The tarantula scrambled around inside, lunging at the translucent sides with its fangs bared. "Magazine!" Michael floundered his free hand behind him. "Magazine, now!"

Corey shoved the magazine at him. Michael slipped it under the edge of the counter and scooted the Tupperware until the top was covered by the magazine. Once the tarantula was secure, he turned toward the sliding glass door. Janice dove out of the way, skillet poised like a shield, and pulled Corey with her. *There*. Michael darted into the backyard, ignoring Janice's shout—*toss it over the fence!*—and Corey's defensive sigh—*I could've handled it*—and set the Tupperware in the grass on the far side of the house. He glanced at the tall wall, climbing up and up to the pointed top where the attic window perched.

"You must be Lizzy," Michael grumbled. He took a step back and toed the magazine away.

The tarantula skittered over the edge of the plastic. It lunged at Michael once, legs swiping at the air, then ran into the bushes and began scaling the wall. Once all eight legs rounded the edge that led to the front of the house, Michael walked back inside.

Janice glared at him. "We could've just killed it."

"I took care of it," Michael said. "It's over, done, no more spider. Happy?"

"How the hell did it get in the house?" She blew a stray piece of hair out of her face.

Corey shrugged. "Maybe through the vents?"

"Well, I'm calling an exterminator," she said. Her mouth thinned and she whipped the skillet back and forth, gesturing between Corey and Michael. "Head count for the party yet?"

"I invited a few friends and they're inviting a few friends," Corey said.

Michael rolled his eyes. "Since the spider crisis is averted, I'm going back to bed. Cool? Cool."

"No, not cool. We need to spider-proof this house before we fill it with people!" Janice's voice grew louder the farther Michael got. He made it all the way to the top of the stairs before she snapped, "Michael Desmond Gates!"

"You sound like Mom," he called back.

The attic door popped open. He glanced over his shoulder before stepping inside, and found Victor, dressed in a T-shirt and jeans, pacing back and forth in front of the bed. He halted when Michael locked the door, frown carved into his face.

"Where is she?" Victor asked, eyes darting to Michael's hands.

"The spider?"

"Pink zebra tarantula," he corrected sternly.

Michael snorted. He opened his mouth to speak, but a shadow scrambled over the edge of the open window before he could. He made the shape of a gun with his hand and pointed. "Is that her?"

Victor whipped around. "*Elizabeth*," he said, elated and surprised, and maybe a bit irritated. "Where the hell have you been?" He rushed to the window and opened his palm, allowing her to crawl into his hand. She climbed his forearm, over his elbow and settled on his shoulder. He tried to look at her and sighed, plucking her back into his hand instead. "I was worried about you, you little asshole." Elizabeth lifted her front legs and bared her fangs. "Put your teeth away, I'm serious. It's been a year, Lizzy. A whole fucking year."

*He's talking to the spider.* Michael lifted a brow. *I'm sleeping with a demon who talks to spiders.*

Victor stroked her back with two fingers. "Elizabeth, this is Michael—Michael, this is my familiar, Elizabeth. You can call her Lizzy."

Michael's lips parted. His forehead wrinkled as he tried to conceal the confusion that tightened his jaw and hardened his eyes. "Elizabeth," he tested. "Your... familiar?"

"My companion. When a witch is born, a piece of their spirit buries itself in an animal. Elizabeth was born when I was born, she'll die when I die. So, yes, a familiar."

"She's the Salem to your Sabrina," Michael said. He watched Lizzy step onto Victor's shoulder again. "Right?"

"Something like that."

"And she's been missing, is that it?"

"I thought she was gone," Victor said. Lizzy settled close to his neck. A small smile twitched onto his face. "When my heart stopped, Allocer went forward with the integration and she just... She was gone. I couldn't find her anywhere."

"Well, she found my sister and my roommate, and they were two seconds away from beating her to death with last month's *Cosmopolitan*, so."

"She wouldn't hurt anyone," Victor snapped.

"I'm sure she wouldn't, but nobody likes spiders, Victor."

"She's a tarantula."

"She's a big, furry spider. If Janice sees her again, she might not make it out with all her legs."

Victor sighed. He rifled through his nightstand instead of answering. "I need to find out where you've been," he muttered. A sleek black phone was unearthed, small and thin in Victor's big hand. "Vassa," he whispered, eyes narrowed at the screen. "Not Vassa." Another annoyed swipe with his thumb. "There you are."

"You have a phone?" Michael tilted his head.

"No, I use carrier pigeons," Victor said, sarcasm heavy over each syllable.

"I've never seen you use a phone! Not once!"

"That's because I don't use it often. Doesn't mean I don't have one."

"Texting happens to be a thing people who get naked together do sometimes," Michael said.

Victor snorted, eyes flicking to Michael before they swept back to the screen. "Are we fighting? Is this our first fight?"

"No," Michael spat, cheeks hot and chest tight. *But having your number might make this a little more normal.* "Sorry, I just don't get it."

"Get what? Me having a phone?"

"No, you being a demon but also having a witch's familiar. That's what I'm not getting. The secret phone is just an added bonus."

"It wasn't a secret." Victor's brows lifted. "And I don't get why Lizzy disappeared and suddenly reappeared either. That's what I'm trying to figure out." His phone buzzed. Golden eyes narrowed at the screen, teeth worrying his bottom lip. "Vassa doesn't know how it happened," he whispered, defeated. He tilted his head to look at Lizzy. "Where've you been, huh?"

Michael nodded to himself. It was strange, this house, this thing he'd started with Victor, this town and the people who called it home. He didn't know what to do, how to react to things like tarantulas in his kitchen or knowing a necromancer had stood in the place he was currently standing.

Witches were real. Necromancers were real. Magic was probably still inside him, pressed into his skin by Victor's hands and body.

"I need a shower," Michael blurted. He didn't know what else to say. *I'm glad your spider isn't being scrubbed off the kitchen counter? Congratulations on scaring the shit out of my sister?*

Victor's sigh was probably followed by *wait* or *hold on,* but Michael closed the door before he heard what he said.

The steps creaked under his feet. Corey peeked around the edge of his open bedroom door and startled, glancing at Michael, the attic door, at Michael again.

"We aren't allowed in there," Corey said.

Michael nodded. "I thought I heard something. I was just checking it out."

"Isn't the door locked?"

"Yeah, it is. I was... I was just..." Michael chewed on the inside of his cheek. "The landlord left us keys in case we needed to check the window jams. Don't worry about it."

Nautical eyes gave him a once-over, pausing for too long over his stomach. Michael thought he might be able to see remnants from last night, bruises or come or hickeys or red marks from Victor's claws. But Corey swallowed uncomfortably, and Michael realized the thick, palpable silence wasn't brought on by his secret relationship, but by the scars lining his hipbones and laddering his ribs.

"Ouch," Corey whispered. He feigned playfulness and attempted a smile, gesturing to the jagged scab on his hip. "That one looks new."

"I slipped," Michael said, plucking an excuse from the neatly stored lineup he had memorized in the back of his mind. *I slipped. Pet a mean cat. Cut myself shaving.* "I'm fine."

"You are, yeah," Corey said. Michael didn't catch the joke until Corey's smile turned into a bold laugh. "That was *awful*, wow, I'm—shit. I'm sorry."

"You're horrible at flirting," Michael said. He desperately wanted to cover the marks on his body. Not because he was embarrassed, but because Corey's inquisitive gaze kept crawling over them, inspecting and prodding.

"Yeah, I'm not very gifted in that department."

He scrubbed a hand over the back of his head and stepped into the bathroom. His stomach was in knots, skin flushed and tongue clumsy. *Don't make eye contact.* Michael shifted his gaze to the floor. "You excited for the party?"

"Yeah, you?"

"Should be fun as long as I don't have to save another spider," Michael said. He bit back a small smile and braved another glance at Corey's face.

"Let me kill it next time." Corey winked. *He winked.* "Then you can thank me for saving you the trouble."

Michael's mouth squirmed, stretching into a wider smile. He rolled his eyes, slipped behind the door and closed it. Corey was definitely flirting with him. Not playful *we're-both-Queer-this-is-fun* flirting. He was *I-want-to-bend-you-over-a-bed* flirting. No questions asked. No mistaking it. He cursed under his breath and tipped his head back against the door, sharp pain tingling in his lip where he bit down.

This was complicated. Unnecessarily, ridiculously complicated.

Not because Michael was dating someone else, but because he didn't know how to politely tell Corey that casual sex between roommates was a terrible idea. For one, because Corey would probably convince him otherwise, and two, because he was sleeping with their *other* roommate anyway—the magical one, the demonic one, the one Corey didn't know existed.

Hot water sprayed, drowning out any sound beyond the bathroom door. He stepped in the shower and placed his palms against the wall. Heat rushed over his bare skin. Thoughts of last night cycled through him, turning and turning. Victor's gentleness. How he'd touched Michael's scars reverently, the way he'd pleaded with him from the backyard when his damn familiar was in danger.

God, Michael was in way too deep.

The lights flickered. He saw Victor appear near the counter, his silhouette stretched by steam, and watched him strip through the fogged shower door. Victor paused, hand hovering over the handle, and said, "Do you want to be alone?"

"I don't want to talk about your spider or your ex-necromancer," Michael said. He realized how catty he sounded a second too late. He winced, scolding himself, but stayed quiet.

"That's not an answer."

"I don't know my place in any of this, Victor. I'm just—"

"Nobody is *just* anything." Victor manifested in front of him, lashes long and eyes dark, body suddenly crowding against his own. Clawed hands curled over Michael's hips and pressed him into the shower wall. "I know my situation isn't easy for you, but it's all I know."

"I know that." Bravery seeped to the top of Michael's skin. He looped his arms over Victor's shoulders and tilted his head, wrapping his fingers around the back of both horns. "This happened really fast."

"This?"

"Us. We happened really fast."

"Do you want to slow down?" Victor's voice lowered, lips teasing the shell of his ear.

"No, that's not what I want."

Teeth grazed his throat. "Then tell me what you want, Michael."

Michael's eyes slipped shut. He curled his leg around Victor's waist. Claws followed the curve of his thigh. *Tell me what you want.* He wanted a lot of things. He wanted to know everything about Victor's life. He wanted to know about magic, and Elizabeth, and Vassa, and the clans. He wanted it to mean something when he bled.

"I want you to show me," Michael whispered. He dropped his hands to Victor's shoulders and pressed down. "I want you to show me magic and witchcraft and—" A soft gasp cut the rest of what he was going to say in half.

Victor pressed his lips to Michael's chest and stomach, dropped to his knees and licked across the wound on his hip, then lifted one of his legs until it was over his shoulder and said, "All you had to do was ask."

He clutched Victor's horns again, leaning heavily on the wall as water dripped over his shoulders and arms and stomach. Victor's mouth was hot and wet. He let Michael pull on him, relaxed his jaw and moaned when Michael's hips jerked.

"I want you to..." *Cut me. Leave marks. Tell me everything.* His abdomen flexed and his breath came short. Victor opened his eye and looked up at him, nose snug against his pelvis, tongue working the underside of his cock. "Fuck, Vic, you're stunning," Michael purred, choking back a moan before it echoed through the bathroom.

Victor kept his eyes open, even when he winced, even when Michael tugged on his horns and forced his cock deeper, even when Michael held him in place and came in his mouth without warning. After Michael's hands slid away from his horns, Victor stood, water catching on his messy lips, eyes narrowed and glowing under the fluorescent lights.

"What do you want?"

"I want you to use me," Michael said softly. He bit his lip—a small surge of pain to ground him.

Victor didn't move.

"I'm giving you permission to use me," Michael clarified. He leaned closer, dragging his lips over Victor's chin, teeth hooked over his jaw, scraping their way to his ear. "Fuck me like you own me."

It happened quickly. Painfully. Victor flipped Michael around and forced his chest against the wall. Michael's heart pounded. He spread his legs, but Victor kicked them further apart. Teeth sank into his shoulder, his neck, stung on his ear lobe. "Safe word."

"Seriously?"

"Seriously."

"Tulip," Michael sneered. But he held on to the way the word fit on his tongue, how it came out sharp and delicate. He didn't want to use it. He probably wouldn't. But he might.

The thought struck him when Victor bit him again, hard, harder. *Tulip* was clenched between his teeth as a cap clicked and Victor rubbed the pads of his clawed fingers between his legs. He didn't take his time. Victor spread lube over his hole and pulled on his hips. He forced Michael to lift his heels and balance on the balls of his feet. His cock was blunt, and the impact of his hipbones on a sudden, rushed thrust knocked the breath from Michael's lungs. That was what he'd wanted. Gracelessness. Mean, violent intimacy that tasted like *fight*.

Michael wanted rough. He wanted pain and release and sex that felt like being torn apart. He was angry, somehow. Angry and human and lost in a situation he barely understood. "Harder," he whimpered, trying to keep his voice low, muffled by the running water.

Victor pinned his arms above his head, wrists clenched in one hand. He growled, animalistic and dark, the sound mingling with their skin meeting again and again, and Michael's quick, short breaths.

Janice yelled from the hallway. "You're gonna use up all the hot water, asshole!"

Victor ground into him, one hand on Michael's lower back, pressing down, opening his spine, encouraging his body to make room and squeeze tight.

"Don't stop," Michael said, resting his temple on the shower wall. He squeezed his eyes shut and fought back another steep moan.

Lips touched the place between his shoulder blades. Victor fucked him hard and fast. His body didn't know what to do with the sensations. He was overwhelmed—aching and tender and suddenly powerless. Like this, with his hands pinned and Victor inside him, his brutal pace and vise grip, Michael was truly out of control.

"Can you come again?" Victor nipped his shoulder.

The idea made his head spin. He gasped and shook his head, but he wanted to, *fuck*, he wanted to.

Victor reached around and took Michael's oversensitive cock in his hand. Every touch sent barbed pleasure jolting into his stomach and chest.

"Are you sure about that?" Victor's voice was a thousand whispers.

He managed not to cry out when Victor shoved him harder against the wall, but tears edged the corner of his eyes and were swept away by the lukewarm water. Michael's second orgasm rolled through him, unsteady and rigid, like it'd been ripped from him before he could process it. He flinched and went limp, deliriously wrung out and too dazed to stay tense. Subspace was comfortable like this—malleable and simplified. It left Michael in the place where his body was not completely his anymore. Victor's pace didn't slow. He used Michael's body until his hips finally stuttered, snug against his ass, and he came inside him, holding him in place as he ground in deep, claws like five blades digging into his thigh. A whispered curse was muffled into the back of Michael's neck. Teeth sank into the place where his neck met his shoulder. Hard. *Harder*. Stinging, hot pain rippled through his skin. Victor kept him there, caged and suspended, with his muscles flexed and fluttering, tracking the drip of slick heat crawling down the back of his thighs. After another sharp exhale, his grip on Michael's wrists loosened. Breath came easier. Michael eased his feet onto the shower floor.

"You okay?" Victor sounded like himself again. He rested his horns against Michael's shoulder.

Legs wobbling, hips aching, Michael covered a wince with his arm. Victor stepped back and placed his palms on Michael's waist, taking some of his weight as he turned and tipped his head against the wall.

"Seriously, Michael!" Janice yelled.

Water sprayed down on them. Victor's hands were featherlight on his skin, his body inches away, leaving a sliver of space between them. Michael didn't know what to say. Yeah, he was okay—*of course* he was okay. But his body betrayed him. Legs shook and knees buckled, pain bloomed low in his back and unfurled in his hips. Usually he was alone for this part. The recovery part. The part that came after. When the possessive sex he craved left him unsteady and aching. The part where he was too emotional and numb to talk.

"C'mon," Victor whispered. He guided Michael's arms over his shoulders, held him close, and didn't move when Michael clung to him. He pushed his face into the space between Victor's neck and shoulder, hummed when Victor ran soapy palms over his back, between his legs, across his stomach. "Nod if you're okay."

Michael nodded.

"Can you walk?"

He snorted and pressed his lips to Victor's neck, voice soft and raspy. "Yeah, I can walk. Don't flatter yourself."

Suds circled the drain by their feet. Once they were both lathered and scrubbed and clean, Victor turned off the water and opened the shower door. He took Michael's hands, fingers curled delicately over his knuckles, and watched him step onto the tile.

Michael's pupils were dilated, his breathing shallow and body loose. Despite the way pain throbbed in him—a delicious, familiar sensory comfort—Michael would've done whatever Victor said right then. Being this deep in subspace for the first time in months with someone he *actually* trusted was unnerving.

"You're shaking," Victor whispered.

"Adrenaline." A simple answer for a simple assessment.

"Do you want to be alone?"

Michael's eyes widened. His top lip peeled away from the bottom one. "No, but if you do—"

"I'll meet you in your room." Victor vanished. Wisps of translucent gray smoke curled toward the bulbs above the mirror.

Folded towels were stuffed in a cubby attached to the shelves beside the toilet. He took one, holding it for a moment as the mirror cleared, and gave his reflection a once-over. Glassy, dark eyes looked back at him. His cheeks were blotched red, shoulder shadowed by mouth-shaped bruises. Prints from Victor's fingers darkened his hips and bloody pinpricks beaded on the soft skin where claws had pierced his thigh. He placed his hands on the counter and let his knees buckle for a second, weight held by shaking arms and white knuckles.

He'd been doing this for a long time. Sex was easy. Power was easy. But mixing those two things with the urge to know and be known was difficult. *Deep breaths.* He inhaled and exhaled, blinking the wetness from his eyes, and carefully wrapped the towel around his waist. When he walked into his bedroom, Victor would be there. Michael wasn't going to get dressed and slip away. He wasn't going to drink a glass of water and make fleeting eye contact while anxiety bubbled inside him. He wasn't going to run.

Christian's voice splintered from a distant memory. *You're really leaving.* He'd had his fingers wrapped around Michael's throat, not squeezing, just there—a reminder. *You'll remember me, right?* He'd snorted a line of white powder off Michael's stomach and fucked him like he was unbreakable. *I'll make sure you remember me.* Christian hadn't kissed him, not once. When it ended, Michael had been left shaking and raw on a bed he didn't belong in next to a man who wouldn't look at him with the words *get out* ringing loud in his ears.

Michael swatted a tear off his cheek.

"Hey, man, is there hot water left? Janice is pitching a fit." Corey knocked politely on the bathroom door.

"Yeah," he blurted and cleared his throat. "Just give it a few minutes to warm back up. Shouldn't be long."

"You okay?"

Michael looked at his reflection again and saw the person he'd left in Arizona staring back at him. A razor blade pressed to his arm in a pearl bathroom, scented like Dior, with lipstick that wasn't his smeared over his cheek and Christian's touch still stinging on his skin. "Yeah, I'm..." He inhaled a long, slow breath. "I'm fine." Corey's shadow shifted at the bottom of the door. He lingered, waiting, but eventually left, footsteps light as he crossed the hall.

"You're fine," Michael whispered to his reflection. He brushed his teeth. Moisturized. Rubbed antiseptic over the scab on his hip. Dabbed ChapStick on his lips. *Breathe.* Put two fingers to the raised bite mark on his shoulder. *Keep breathing.*

The hall was empty, but Corey's bedroom door was open. He glanced inside. Posters lined the far wall above a small bed and a guitar was propped against the nightstand. Corey stood just inside the door, his wandering eyes scaling Michael's bare chest.

"You comin' to school?" Corey asked. Concern formed a thin smile on his face and furrowed his brows.

Michael shook his head. "I've gotta work today, but there's a drop-in for a Horticulture Lab on Monday."

"You sure you're okay?"

"Yeah, I'm okay—I'm good," he said.

Corey nodded. He offered another smile before Michael darted into his room and locked the door behind him. The air rippled. He wanted to crumble, to find the solace he usually did in being flayed open. But instead, he was raw and tender, heart still kicking hard, emotions fractured where memories and magic went to war inside him. *This isn't your world*, fear said. Courage rang louder. *But it could be.*

Victor stood next to the balcony, dressed and manicured, with his gaze fixed on Michael. "We should relax for a minute," he said softly. "You seem..."

*Weak.*

The thought caused his knees to shake again. One leg buckled. He tried to catch himself on the dresser, but Victor was there before he could. His hands were suddenly on Michael's waist, voice gentle and lulling. "C'mon," Victor said. His pupils narrowed into catlike diamonds. He shifted, and they crossed the room in one step. Energy pulsed and hummed, bending to Victor's will. He eased Michael onto the edge of the bed. Everything moved too quickly. Victor was there, holding him, then he was on the bed, blinking back confusion as Victor knelt by his feet.

"What're you doing?" Michael blushed, following Victor's silent command as he tapped his foot, signaling for him to lift it.

Victor tossed the damp towel aside and helped him into a pair of clean gym shorts. "Taking care of you."

"You don't have to."

"I want to."

"Victor—"

"Have you experienced sub drop before?" His golden eyes flicked to Michael's face.

Michael swallowed hard. He gave a curt shake of his head.

"Do you know what it is?"

"I've heard of it, but I mean... I found subspace, I was fine, I..."

Another flutter of magic. Another sudden gust. Michael barely felt his body lift. His back sank into the bed and Victor laid down beside him, arm curled lightly over his waist. Everything inside him reached for a plausible explanation, a way to debunk how Victor had moved him from one place to the next in the blink of an eye. But rather than entertain unanswerable questions, Michael pressed closer to Victor's chest.

"Sub drop can happen in a lot of different ways for a lot of different reasons," Victor said. He kept his voice low and even and dragged his claws soothingly up and down Michael's back.

"It's not like you tied me up and flogged me," Michael muttered. He hid his face beneath Victor's chin and followed each breath he took. "Or cut me, or spanked me, or choked me... We just—it wasn't..." Speech failed him.

"Was it intense for you?"

"Fuck off, c'mon," he whined.

"Is that a yes?"

Michael's cheeks burned hotter and he nodded.

"Are you tired? A little off-kilter?"

Michael nodded again.

"Sub drop can happen when a sudden rush of endorphins and adrenaline have no sensory stimulation to respond to. It's a sort of shock you go through, like jumping in a cold lake after a hot shower. We were intense, you found subspace, and once the intensity ended, your emotional and physical responses went a little off the charts. It happens." Victor pressed his lips to the top of Michael's head. "Does that make sense?"

"You're so textbook," Michael said. "Sounds like you've been in this situation before."

"A couple times."

Michael snaked his arm around Victor's shoulder. "Sorry I'm such a dick about everything."

"You know that I enjoyed myself, right?" Victor brought their bodies closer. Their legs tangled. Michael cracked his eyes open and nodded. "Did you enjoy yourself?" Goose bumps followed Victor's claws.

He slid his thigh between Victor's legs, snuggling closer. "Yeah, I did."

Victor hummed contentedly. He hooked his fingers around Michael's jaw and tilted his head back to catch his gaze. "Thank you for trusting me like that. Is there anything you need?"

Never had a partner, a lover, a one-night-stand—*no one*—asked him a question like that in a situation like this. Michael didn't know what to do with it. He didn't know how to answer or respond, if he should laugh or cry or hide under the comforter.

*Food*, he thought, then immediately reconsidered. Water, maybe. *This*, he decided, and kissed Victor on the lips.

"Nap with me," Michael said against his mouth. He decided to tell the truth. To ask for things. To accept blatant affection when it was being offered. "Keep tickling my back. Have lunch with me when we wake up."

"I can do that." Victor kissed him again, deeper, longer. Things between them were still heated enough to pull a quiet moan from Michael's chest, and he shivered when Victor broke away to breathe against his lips. "You felt so fucking good," Victor whispered and tilted his head to accommodate another kiss. Michael opened his mouth, breath hot between their parted lips. "I'd make another deal with the devil for the chance to keep you close."

His hips were starting to ache. The pleasant warmth and numbness of his afterglow faded, leaving him tangled in sub drop, needy and brittle and tame in Victor's arms.

Michael kissed him, their lips lazy and patient, pressing and parting for the wet slide of tongues and nip of teeth. "I'm not going anywhere," Michael said.

Victor pulled him close, cradling the back of his head with one hand and trailing his claws lightly over Michael's skin with the other. His breath was steady, nose buried in Michael's hair.

Birds chirped to welcome the morning and Michael fell asleep to the sound of Victor's steady heartbeat, wondering about magic and pain, and asking himself questions he never had before.

Did healing feel like this?

Was he someone who needed to heal?

MICHAEL SMOKED A cigarette after their mid-morning nap. He let the balcony wall take most of his weight and looked out over the trees. Water dripped from the drainpipes on the roof. The sky was blue in some places and gray in others, smudged with more dark clouds rolling in from the sea.

Janice had texted him to complain about his long showers. Corey had followed him on Instagram. The party was tomorrow, and Michael didn't know if he was ready for a house full of people. For drinking games and music. For Janice to tell people stories about their days in high school or for her to point at Michael's phone and say *show them that picture I like from St. Paul's Cathedral!* He took a drag, the filter hot between his fingers, and dropped the cigarette butt in a watery ashtray.

Cabinets opened and closed downstairs. Victor had wandered into the kitchen to make them lunch and now the house was scented with maple and rosemary, bacon and eggs. Something sizzled. Something else cracked. Michael's gaze skimmed the treetops, their leaves stained orange and violet and crimson.

There was a guy downstairs cooking for him. The same guy who had baked brownies for him, the same guy who had stacked chairs on top of the kitchen table to get his attention and fucked him better than anyone ever had and made the idea of a relationship seem enticing instead of awful. Victor Lewellyn was downstairs. The demon who had woken Michael from their nap by thumbing gently at his cheekbone and pressing his lips to the bridge of Michael's nose.

Life had never been more interesting or frightening.

Michael pulled a sweatshirt over his head and snatched his laptop case from the nightstand. He had a blog post to write today and his followers on Instagram were getting antsy for new content. If he didn't post something every other day, add to his story or touch base with travel websites, he could lose sponsorships. But his blog and his followers would have to wait because whatever Victor was cooking smelled in-fucking-credible.

"You're not a vegetarian, right?" Victor asked. He tipped his head back to look at Michael, watching as he slid into a chair at the kitchen table.

Michael shook his head. "No, but I can't do a lot of red meat." His nostrils flared and his nose twitched. "Bacon?"

"It's turkey bacon." Victor arched a brow and grinned, gesturing from the skillet with the bacon to the plated chicken breasts resting on the counter. "Rosemary chicken sandwiches. You want a fried egg on yours?"

"Yeah, if you've already got the eggs out."

"Avocado?"

Michael shifted nervously. His eyes flicked from Victor to the stove, from the stove to the fridge. "Sure, if it's okay."

"Why wouldn't it be okay?"

"Because you're the one cooking. I eat what you put in front of me, that's kinda the deal here."

"It definitely isn't," Victor said. He pulled the bacon strips off the skillet and cracked an egg. "I wouldn't expect you to eat something you didn't like. I offered to cook, so I'm cooking. Doesn't mean you're obligated to like it."

He averted his gaze to the table. Simple things like this—brunch on a weekday after falling back into bed together—made Michael realize how much he'd missed. All the time he'd spent keeping his distance from something as absurdly easy as this made him wonder if it would last. Him. Victor. What they'd found in each other.

The quiet was pulled tight, tense and watched.

"Romaine or spinach?" Victor asked. His voice was calm and patient, as if he saw the apprehension festering in Michael and wanted to soothe it.

"Spinach," Michael said.

"Mustard?"

"Please."

"Swiss?"

Michael chewed on the inside of his lip. "Don't we have Gouda?"

"I think I saw some. Gouda, then?"

"Yeah, if…" Michael paused. Victor glanced at him, brows lifted, a playful smile twitching on his mouth. He sighed and said, "Yeah, thanks."

Victor plucked browned sourdough slices from the toaster. Michael wanted to watch him, but that was weird, wasn't it? Watching someone cook? He rolled his eyes, irritated at himself, and opened his laptop. His stomach growled. The house was silent except for Victor moving around the kitchen and Michael's fingers on the keys.

"Shit, seriously?" Michael said under his breath. He skimmed an e-mail from the brand ambassador he'd contacted two weeks ago and snorted. "Do I look like someone who would carry around a camo backpack?"

Two plates were set on the table and Victor took the seat beside him, leaning over to peek at the screen. "Not really. Why? What's that?"

"My contact at REI said they'll offer me sponsorship if I use that heinous thing as my hiking pack. Like, I have to photograph myself going places with it which means I have to be seen in public with it."

"It's not *that* bad," Victor said, but his voice was strained through his teeth—a polite nicety.

He pushed his laptop aside and pulled the plate toward him. The sandwich was cut in half, perfectly assembled, and looked as good as it smelled. He propped his elbows on the table and grabbed one half. "Next they'll want me to wear a MAGA hat and pose in the bed of a lifted truck."

"I highly doubt that," Victor said through a laugh.

"Uh huh, we'll see." Michael reached over with his free hand to switch tabs on the screen. He glanced at Victor, offering a faint smile, then took a bite, chewed, paused, and narrowed his eyes. "This is the best sandwich I've ever eaten," he said, annoyed. "And you stood here, like that—" he gestured to Victor's unbuttoned black shirt, the exposed bronze skin beneath, and his snug jeans "—and whipped it together like it was nothing."

"I put chicken on bread, Michael. It wasn't rocket science."

"I've burned ramen before," Michael said, as if that should explain his surprise. "And I'm pretty sure my attempt at mashed potatoes almost ended in a house fire."

Victor's laughter was genuine and full. His lips split, pushing dimples into his cheeks and crinkling the skin around his eyes. He looked younger right then, in the middle of a bold laugh with a sandwich in one hand, illuminated by muted daylight that brightened the kitchen. He took a bite, cheek stuffed full of food, and rolled his eyes. "I've been cooking since I was a kid. It comes naturally, I guess."

"What's your favorite thing to make?" Michael tucked a stray piece of spinach between the toasted bread.

"Pies," Victor said.

"Okay, so what's your favorite pie to make?" He finished the first half of the sandwich and licked his fingers clean. It was an unnecessary display, sucking crumbs and avocado from his fingertips, but he liked the way Victor's attention never wavered.

"Banana cream. I make it every summer—vanilla bean, ripe bananas, and honeycomb in a graham cracker crust. Luther lets me harvest the honey straight from the Darbonne hives." He shook his head and his smile quieted. "He used to, at least."

"Luther?"

"Yeah, an old friend of mine. His sister is the newly appointed Darbonne matriarch, I guess."

Michael nodded. The conversation withered after that. They finished eating and Michael stood to fill a glass with orange juice. He wanted to ask Victor to make him a pie sometime. He wanted to tell him life was too short to let his dreams slip away, but then he remembered that life wasn't short for Victor; he had already cheated death and outgrown his humanity. Horns cast thin shadows across Victor's face and his claws looked awkwardly out of place tapping the space bar on Michael's silver laptop.

"You have twenty-two thousand followers," Victor deadpanned.

"People like to see where I go." Michael placed the dishes in the sink before he sat down again, gaze fixed on Victor's eyes as they wandered from one photo to the next. Victor clicked on one post and grinned, snorting through a laugh. It was a picture from Amsterdam. Michael was seated in front of a fountain with a joint pressed between his lips. He scrolled and clicked on another, Stonehenge, and another, Westminster Abbey. "The hostel I stayed at in London was pretty cool. I met some interesting people there."

"You look happy." Victor scrolled until he found a picture of Michael sucking a shot glass out of someone's stomach. "And entertained."

A soft laugh fluttered over his lips. "I don't even remember his name," he mumbled. "But I do remember us not being able to understand each other."

"Did the language barrier stop you?"

"Course not."

They laughed again. Genuine, heartfelt laughter that made wings stir in his chest and heat rush into his cheeks. Victor kept his eyes on the screen, dancing between each square photo. Michael kept his eyes on Victor.

"Does it bother you?" Michael blurted. The question was there, snapping at his confidence, and stumbled out.

"Your Instagram?"

"That I've slept with a lot of people."

Victor jerked his head back as if he'd been slapped. "I hate to break it to you, but I'm not a blushing virgin."

"It doesn't mean you have to be comfortable with my..." He remembered what Victor had said while they were in bed together. "Laundry list of lovers. Most people wouldn't be, and I wouldn't blame you for thinking I'm... I mean, I know what I am—I know what I did, and I—"

"Don't do that, don't turn what I said into a weapon." Victor took Michael's chin between two fingers. "What you *are*? And what exactly is that? Because from where I'm standing, you're a guy who prefers plants to people and successfully turned his passion into a business. Or am I missing something?"

Michael felt the words stir on his tongue. Labels. Insults thrown at him in Christian's bed, ripped from Janice's mouth, whispered by strangers. *Plaything. Whore. Slut.* "Look, you're a good guy, but just about everyone else would think I'm a used-up chew toy."

Victor tugged on his chin. He brought Michael closer, pupils expanding and shrinking. The air froze—a caught kind of stillness that animals perfected in the face of a predator. The gold in his eyes shone brighter. His voice deepened, layered with sparks and hisses and demonic growls. "I'm not everyone else," he said and kissed Michael on the lips. "You're not used up. You're not a chew toy." His breath gusted Michael's chin, warm and familiar. "And I give absolutely zero fucks about your sexual track record. Okay?"

Michael's first instinct was to snap at him. *You don't know what I've done to myself.* To seethe and bite. *You don't know how many people spent years looking for something inside me that you've found in a week.* But he didn't. "You're pretty soft for a demon, you know that?"

Victor kissed him again. He tilted his head, claws sharp on Michael's jaw. "And you're pretty insecure for someone who gets off on regularly scheduled power trips."

"Hey, wow, easy," Michael said, but he laughed. Because, despite the anger flaring inside him, it was the truth. "I get it. I hear you."

"Good."

The conversation ended with another quick kiss.

Victor racked dishes in the dishwasher while Michael updated his blog and responded to overdue e-mails from brand ambassadors. A company wanted him to use their hydro flask. Another person asked about his passport holder. A luggage company and a small business that created travel journals asked for ad space on his website's sidebar.

Once he was caught up on e-mails, Michael opened the drafted blog post he'd been hired to write, added foodie pictures, selfies, plugged a few sponsors, and sent it to his editor.


THE NEXT COUPLE of days blurred together.

Michael managed to write pieces on three different hostels, discussed the history of druid magic and Stonehenge with Victor over fresh baked muffins, and went on a hike through the nearby woods where he took pictures of himself in a brand name snapback for his Instagram. The night before the party, he played Cards Against Humanity with Janice and Corey and wished he could've invited Victor to join them. They nursed beers while MTV played in the background, laughing and kicking and hollering until the game devolved into story-telling rather than question-asking.

At one point, Corey looked at Michael and arched a brow. "Who did that?" He gestured to the place where his sweater dropped, exposing the curve of his freckled shoulder, darkened by an opaque hickey.

"Oh, I ran into a door," Michael said.

"A door with teeth?"

Janice choked on her beer. "He didn't tell you?" She nudged Corey with her elbow, seated beside him on their yellow couch. "He's screwing the poltergeist."

Michael tried not to look too comfortable with the idea.

Corey shook his head. "Seriously, who's the lucky guy?"

"*Lucky guy?*" Janice squawked. She tipped a bottle against her lips and swallowed the rest of her beer. "You mean *poor guy*. Hasn't Michael told you? He's allergic to commitment."

"Fuck you," Michael snapped.

Janice didn't bat an eye. She kept her narrowed gaze fixed on Corey, grin wide and wicked. "Besides, you're not really his type. No ring, no partner—no dice."

Michael shifted his jaw back and forth. "You're in rare form tonight, Jan."

She shot him a hard glare, a warning. He knew that look. He'd seen it over and over again, at parties and bars and weddings and bonfires. *Don't lead him on.* "I'm your big sister," she said, leveling her voice. "It's my job to tease you."

A door on the second floor slammed. The windows trembled. The sound of something heavy scraped across the wall—a large, clawed hand.

Janice and Corey both jumped in their seats. Michael didn't move.

"The poltergeist I've seduced is probably lonely." Michael's tone dripped sarcasm. He stood, grabbed another beer from the fridge, and walked upstairs. "I'll make sure the windows are latched."

Janice and Corey called after him. *Hey, come on, don't be like that! It was a joke! Michael!*

But he disappeared into the attic anyway.

Victor appeared from the shadows, standing tall beside the bookshelf. He flicked his wrist and Michael's feet lifted from the floor. He hovered there, suspended, then slowly drifted toward Victor. His pulse thrummed fast in his veins. Magic slithered around them, tickling his skin, causing his breath to catch and his lungs to ache.

"You were right," Victor whispered. "I was lonely."

Darkness shrouded the room, fractured by a candle sparking to life on the dresser. Then another on the windowsill. Michael hovered in front of Victor for a moment, toes barely grazing the wood floor, until the energy shifted and Victor's magic let him go. He stumbled. Victor steadied him.

"You're gonna get found out if you keep making a bunch of noise." Michael glanced from the lit candles to Victor's face. Shadows stretched and bent, elongating the edge of his cheekbones and the line of his nose. "Slamming doors," he teased. "Scratching walls like a pissed-off cat."

Victor smirked and tugged the bottle from between Michael's knuckles. "You wanted out of there as much as I wanted you up here." He took a sip and paused, studying Michael's face for a long, drawn-out moment. "Do you still want to learn?"

"About magic?"

"Yes."

Heat pooled low in his belly. Like this, skin glowing where candlelight touched, Victor looked deadly and sinful. Like this, wrapped in magic with Michael looking up at him, he felt impossible again. Michael nodded. "Yeah, of course I do."

"Then I'll teach you."

They flipped through books. Victor showed him planetary sigils, traced powerful runes over his skin with the tip of his claw, held a flame in his hand and made it dance. Minutes turned to hours. Victor told him stories about full moon parties and Yule festivities, balanced a quartz cluster in his palm, and explained what kind of witch he'd been before he died.

"My magic was rooted in trees and stones. It was solid—tangible. I could always hold onto it even when other things slipped away," Victor said.

Lizzy sat beside a lit candle on the windowsill. Her shadow crawled across the far wall and leaked over the door, jilting whenever her legs twitched atop the tarot deck she perched on.

"Earth magic, huh? Is that what you used to lift me earlier?" Michael was stretched across Victor's bed next to a plethora of open books, balancing the tip of a black-handled knife in the center of his palm.

"No, that was something else."

"Dark magic?"

He nodded.

"Which is the same as blood magic?" Michael's eyes shifted from the blade to where Victor stood in front of the window.

"Blood magic is dark magic, but dark magic isn't always blood magic," Victor said.

Michael looked at him upside down, head tilted over the side of the bed. "That sounds complicated."

"As complicated as it is dangerous."

"Will you show me?"

Victor paused. His shoulders tightened and his body went rigid, breath held, eyes fixed on the moon past the lace curtain. "It's not something I'll be able to show you, it's something you'll experience. You get that, right?"

"Sure, yeah. I get that."

"It could be overwhelming."

"I'll be okay."

"I could hurt you—"

"You won't."

The temperature dropped. Victor vanished and reappeared on the bed, knees poised over Michael's hips, blade pressed to the soft skin below his chin. "Listen to me," he whispered, voice low and grating. Michael held his breath. He went entirely still. "I need you to know how to stop me. I need you to understand what will happen if you say the words out loud that I'm about to say to you. Okay?"

Michael's breath trembled. "Okay."

"Allocer, I command you to relinquish your hold on me," Victor said. He lifted the blade from Michael's neck. "If you say that—if you command the demonic energy living inside me to let go—I'll let go. Do you remember when you asked me if names had power?"

He nodded. Excitement turned into a blurred line, dividing fear from arousal.

"You were right. They do."

"And if I say it, if I say Allocer, I com—"

Victor clapped his palm over Michael's mouth. "I'm trusting you with this, Michael Gates," he snapped. For the first time, Victor sounded afraid. He eased his hand away and held himself above Michael, palms on either side of his shoulders, eyes blazing and strong, pinned to Michael's face. "It's the closest thing to sacred I have. My name. My magic. It's bound to this house and to a demon, and once you taste my blood, it'll be bound to you."

"Bound to me?"

"I'll feel you. You'll feel me. You'll know things you shouldn't, see things you shouldn't. Memories, maybe. Emotions. Secrets."

"I don't have secrets."

"Everybody has secrets." Victor bit the words at Michael's mouth.

"You're already my biggest secret." Michael let bravery drive him. He curled his fingers around the black handle of the blade and guided it to his throat, still clutched in Victor's hand. The cold tip pressed beneath his ear.

The blade left a shallow cut. Michael gasped, the sting a quick and comforting thing.

"People will see that," Victor said.

"I'll put a Band-Aid over it." He tilted his head back and pressed two fingers to the tiny wound. Blood wet his skin. His pulse kicked and floundered.

*This is what killed him*, Michael thought. His nostrils flared and he rubbed warm, coppery blood over his lips. *This is the magic that changed Victor into something else—something powerful.*

Michael wondered what it might do to him.

Victor curled his arm under Michael's back. His lips were light on Michael's cheek, his temple, the top of his ear, touch sure and firm as he let his weight press down, hips between Michael's legs, mouth hovering just below his jaw. Anticipation gnawed on him. Michael wanted to squirm. He wanted to command Victor to do something, anything.

*Touch me. Hold me down.*

"Are you sure?" Victor asked, breath hot against the bloody cut on his neck.

Michael tilted his head to give him more room. "What'll it feel like?"

"It feels different for everyone."

"What do you *think* it'll feel like?"

"Drugs," Victor rasped. He nosed at the skin below the wound, just above his collarbone. "You smell like honey, you taste like honey, you're probably so fucking sweet like this." His voice devolved again, shattering into a thousand different versions of itself. Growls. Whispers. Screams. Hisses. Claws dug into the concave hollow between Michael's shoulder blades. "I'll ask again—are you sure, Michael?"

"I'm sure," he blurted. He said it again, firmer this time, "I'm sure, yes, do it."

Victor didn't hesitate any longer. His tongue laved across the cut and he immediately went rigid. Michael's body jolted beneath him, magic pouring through his skin, hot and vicious and alive. Digging. Clawing. Climbing between bone and looping around veins. Before he could make a sound, images flashed behind his eyes. They were vivid.

Hands around his hips, holding him still. Christian's voice rippling from a memory he'd kept far, far away—*I'd fuck you all day if I could*—and the feeling that came with it, the useless, secret he'd kept locked behind his heart.

Victor's teeth sank into his skin. He bit hard, moaning against Michael's neck, and pulled him closer.

The crack of a palm across Michael's thigh. Voices. Tequila-drenched fingers pushing past his lips. A steepled crown atop a cathedral that caught the sun. Victor's hand on his forearm, his voice, the way he'd said Michael's name the first day they met. Glasses clanking in an Irish pub. How Michael's heart ached whenever Victor looked at him.

"Let me in," Victor said. He licked Michael's neck again. Sat up and hauled Michael with him, holding him close, one palm cradling the nape of his neck, the other sliding over his denim-clad thigh.

"I am," he whimpered. Memories rushed at him. Voices. His traitorous, foolish heart. Scents and tastes and immortalized pain. *Don't*, he thought. *Don't, don't.* But Victor bit down harder. He sucked and licked and kissed, and Michael closed his eyes.

Michael had loved someone. He'd drowned in it—an unwanted mess. But he'd loved Christian all the same. Michael had loved him despite the bruises. He'd loved him despite the cruelty. He'd loved him even after he left him. A year abroad didn't change anything. He came back to the same mouth and the same bed and the same secret.

That love had made him weak. That love had made him mean.

Victor pulled back. His lips grazed Michael's bloody neck, breaths heavy. Dark, heady magic buzzed between them. "Stay with me," he whispered. His grip on Michael's nape tightened. "Don't get lost in things that don't matter anymore."

Magic *did* feel like drugs. Michael's lashes fluttered and his hips rolled in Victor's lap. Waves of delicious, syrupy magic coated the back of his throat and twisted in every flexed muscle and every curled toe. It filled the empty places inside him with something too big for his body. Victor's energy tasted dark. Chaotic. Vicious. Michael wanted to wear it like a coat. He wanted to swallow it.

He tilted his head until Victor's mouth was close enough to catch. Their noses bumped. Victor's horn knocked gently into his temple. Michael took Victor's hand, curled securely around his thigh, and lifted it, guiding Victor's clawed index finger toward his neck. Victor's eyes shone brighter, their whites eaten by burning, moving gold. His pupils thinned into black diamonds. They breathed the same air. Victor barely flinched when Michael pressed on the back of his hand and dragged his claw across copper skin.

Blood crawled slowly down Victor's chest, a thick, dark line Michael watched with eager eyes. He wanted them bare. He wanted them torn at the edges, vulnerable and honest, exposed as the monsters he already knew they both were.

The candles around the room sparked and popped. Flames climbed higher. Michael watched firelight bounce off Victor's shoulders, placed his palm on Victor's cheek, thumb poised over the swell of his bottom lip, then leaned down and kissed the wet, warm cut at the base of Victor's throat.

Michael immediately pressed closer. He sucked in a sharp breath, blood hot and damning on his tongue. No wonder Victor died from this. No wonder other witches outlawed this. Dark magic, blood magic—this magic— defined seduction. His eyes rolled back. Power pulsed in him, throbbing in his spine and between his legs and deep in his chest.

Then the memories filtered through.

A crisp laugh. Victor in front of a mirror, staring at his reflection with Allocer's sigil freshly carved into his chest. A name—*Vassa*. Cookies on a baking sheet. Victor's tongue between Vassa's legs, their pale skin flecked with blood, fingers tangled in his hair, Vassa's gasps broken by whispered Latin.

Victor threaded his fingers through Michael's hair, a mirrored movement from their shared memory, and tugged him into a kiss. They were messy with each other. Blood passed between their lips and breath turned choppy as emotions merged, memories spun inside them, and desire bit at their bones.

The tail end of Victor's death jolted through him. It was a memory and it wasn't. Victor's energy had thrashed and seized. Allocer had crept into his body, a wraith and an assassin, and had torn him apart. Michael felt Victor's surprise. His resistance. Defeat that became acceptance.

"Come back," Victor said, shaky and strained. "Be here with me. Right here."

Michael framed Victor's face in his hands and looked from his fiery eyes to his bloody mouth. "You're like..." There was no term. No description. Victor was like nothing Michael had ever experienced before. "It's like I pulled you from a dream."

"Nightmare," Victor corrected.

"Both."

Victor kissed him again, slowly this time. Their lips were slick with blood. Michael touched the shallow cut on Victor's throat and brought his wet fingers to their mouths, licking blood away and shivering when Victor did the same.

"Focus," Victor whispered. He kissed the corner of Michael's mouth and leaned down to scrape his teeth over the wound on his neck. "Concentrate on me. On the here and now."

"I felt you die," Michael whispered.

"I felt you fall in love."

"Same thing."

Victor shook his head. He held Michael tightly, tongue hot on the throbbing cut on his neck, claws tickling the back of his head and digging into his hip. They shared each other. Michael felt the whiplash of Victor's power inside him. He felt small. Captured. Victor bit down harder and Michael yelped, hips jerking, hands scrabbling for purchase on his shoulders.

*Careful*, he wanted to say. *Slow down.* But he didn't.

Michael endured what they'd turned into. His body responded to memories, emotions, pleasure, soaking up as much as Victor was willing to give. Everything was amplified. Every kiss, every touch, every movement. Victor licked into his mouth. Blood trickled past the seam of their lips. *Too fast.* Michael gasped when his back hit the bed. He heard Victor's low growl, noticed how the air ran from them, how wrongness seeped through the floor and tainted the room.

A sharp claw sliced his collarbone. Michael's back arched off the bed. He reached for more despite the panic building slowly in the pit of his stomach.

"What're you doing?" Michael choked out.

Victor didn't answer. His teeth came down around the fresh cut on his clavicle and he bit, hard, too hard.

He slapped his palm across his own mouth to muffle a shout. Legs flexed and thrashed against the sheets, but Victor had him pinned. He couldn't move. A part of him didn't want to move, but everything else said *run*. He grabbed Victor's horns and held on with a trembling grip.

This was dangerous pleasure. It was unwarranted. Delirious. Addictive and thrilling. But it *hurt*.

Magic, Victor, his teeth, all those memories.

They hurt.

"Vic, please," Michael sobbed. He didn't know what else to do. Victor was pressing kisses to his neck. He had his hand under Michael's shirt, rucked up to his armpits, and there was blood smeared over his pale skin. His body and mind and heart were all fighting for space inside him. Memories had fangs that pierced his skin, and the senseless pleasure Victor stirred within him was too much in ways Michael couldn't parse. *It hurt.* That was the truth. In the end, even the sharp, delicious ache that lived in the space between pain and pleasure—the high Michael chased—was too intense. "Tulip," he blurted. "Tulip, tulip—"

Victor vanished. One moment he'd been there, body hot and strong on top of him, and a second later he was gone. Michael panted. Chills scaled his arms and his chest heaved, jaw slack and mouth quivering. His jeans were low on his hips, button unfasted and zipper pulled down. *Just a memory.* He chanted it to himself. *It was a memory.* Magic lingered.

The floor creaked. Michael followed the sound. He blinked stray tears from his eyes, watching Victor shift from foot to foot in the corner of the room. One clawed hand was curled over his elbow, guarded and apprehensive. Concern furrowed his brow.

"Are you all right?" Victor asked.

Michael closed his eyes. "Come back—I'm sorry, I just—"

"Don't apologize." The candles died, their flames shrinking to an acceptable, natural height. "Did I go too far?"

"I don't know... I just..." Michael inhaled a shaky breath. "Please, come back. Don't just... Don't fucking stand over there like I'm a leper. I'm covered in your blood; I think we're past giving each other space."

"Everyone needs space sometimes. If you—"

"I don't, okay?" Michael hissed. His voice cracked horribly. Something terrible lodged in his throat—a feeling too close to grief to be anything but affection. He covered his face with his hands and took a deep breath, trying and failing to keep it together. Crying wouldn't explain anything. Being pissed wouldn't either. "I don't want space, Vic. I want you to..." He didn't know how to say it. He didn't know if he *could* say it.

The bed dipped when Victor returned. He crawled over Michael, keeping space between them until he was poised above him, bloody and gorgeous and tragic.

Not tragic because of the blood. But because Victor Lewellyn was everything Michael had always wanted, and Michael never wanted a damn thing that ever truly wanted him back.

"I had this weird, childish hope that maybe I would fit somewhere in your world. But your magic? Your death?" Michael exhaled and dropped his hands to the bed, revealing flushed cheeks and watery eyes, glistening lashes and a mouth stained red. "It doesn't make room for people like me. I'm not powerful like you or magical like you—I'm not a witch or a demon or a fucking elf, I'm just..."

"Elves don't live in North America," Victor whispered.

"You know what I mean," Michael said.

"Witches are human, by the way. They're just humans who are born with the natural ability to use magic."

Michael searched his face. He clicked his tongue, annoyed, and licked crusted blood from his bottom lip. "Why the hell are you wasting your time with me? Is it because I'm stuck in this house with you?"

Victor narrowed his eyes. "Yeah, that's exactly why."

He scoffed and rolled his eyes.

"That's what you wanna hear, isn't it? That you're convenient? That I'm not really interested in you, I just like fucking you. Right? That's what you're used to?"

Silence filled the space between them. Michael chewed on his lip and averted his gaze, caught in the metal teeth of a very real, very sore truth. Yeah, that's what he was used to. Yeah, that's what he expected. He looked at the place where blood had soaked into white sheets and held his breath.

"You can project all you want, Michael. But I was in your head. I felt your—"

"Then you already know I'm being shitty because I'm scared, so stop."

Victor's lips curved into a smile. He let out a short breath and leaned down to press his lips to Michael's ear. "I like you because you're smart and adventurous and brave, and because you'd probably laugh at a funeral."

Michael huffed out a breath. "You're good, Vic. You're the real deal."

"Good at what?" Victor purred suggestively. He scraped his teeth over Michael's earlobe. "I'd love to hear you say it."

"*This*," Michael said. His blush darkened, lips pressed into a thin line to suppress a smile. "You're good at disarming me. You're good at being nice and accepting people and being patient and, fuck, you're just good, okay? It's irritating."

"Are you actually irritated or are you upset that I saw what I saw? What Christian did was—"

"Don't." Michael's teeth clicked. He pushed at Victor's chest until he could see his face again, pupils still slitted, eyes still overwhelmingly gold. "Don't say his name. Don't *ever* say his name." His voice quaked, whispered and rushed. He swallowed uncomfortably, suddenly too hot, suddenly too nervous. "Please."

Victor's eyes softened. He watched Michael carefully, picking him apart bit by bit. *What a mess*, Michael thought. *I'm such a fucking mess*. But still, Victor leaned down and pressed his lips to Michael's cheek, his chin, his neck. "Tell me what I'm good at," he rasped, nuzzling Michael's throat, coaxing him to tilt his head back and make room.

This was a distraction. A lovely, tender, appreciated distraction.

"You're good at cooking," Michael teased. Victor swept his hand down Michael's side and thumbed at his jeans. "You're good at being stealthy." At that, Victor laughed, smothering it against his shoulder. "You're good at going down on me." Lips touched his bloody collarbone.

"Concentrate on me," Victor said. Another kiss to Michael's chest. "Keep talking."

The hand pawing at his jeans disappeared. Michael closed his eyes, but when he opened his mouth to speak, he found wet fingertips and sharp claws on his tongue. He licked them clean, the taste of Victor's blood strong and acidic. "You're good at making me feel safe," he said. Teeth on his sternum. Lips around his nipple. Magic still tangled inside him. It thrummed and bent, stirring memories and feelings—Victor touching him, Victor's mouth on his cock, Victor's breath on his neck—to seep to the surface. "You're good at…" Michael gasped and grabbed Victor's shoulders. "Making me feel wanted."

"What else?" Victor bit the soft skin below his belly button.

He slid his hands to Victor's face, curled his fingers around the base of his horns, and tugged him back up into a kiss. "You're good at making me bleed," he said. The energy heated this time. Walls closed in and the room tilted, and Michael let himself be pulled under. He wanted to drown in the echoes they shared: Victor's hands on his hips, Michael's throat flexing, Victor's fingers deep inside him, Michael's wrecked breath and soft sounds. Christian was gone. Vassa was gone. The memories they'd kept locked behind heavy doors were back where they belonged.

This magic was theirs.

Michael stripped out of his jeans, then pulled at the hem of Victor's shirt until it was tossed away. He shoved Victor onto his back and crawled over him, lips following hips and ribs, resting above the sigil over his heart. "You're good at making me come."

The night moved slowly. Moonlight didn't cut past the dark clouds outside the window, and candles fizzled out one by one. Smoke curled through the air, scented like jasmine and rose. Michael's shirt was crusted with blood, bunched up around Victor's hand scaling his stomach and chest. He pushed Victor's jeans and boxers to his thighs and snatched the small tube stashed under the pillow. Their eyes stayed locked as Michael pressed two fingers into himself, poised above Victor, on display. Watched. *Seen.*

The house didn't make a sound. All Michael heard was his own soft breaths, choppy and barely there. The bed beneath them shifted as he guided Victor's cock between his legs and sank down, riding him with fluid, steady rolls of his hips. Darkness wrapped around them. Everything was still. Seconds stretched. Minutes felt like eternities. They were half dressed, in bed, making love, if that's what this was, and Michael couldn't look away from him. Victor bucked into him, fingers curled around his hips, and held him down.

"Like that," Victor said through a gentle, low moan.

Michael closed his eyes and circled his hips. He kept Victor deep inside him, nudged against his prostate, right where he needed him most, and let their dark magic move through him.

He relived every touch. Heard every moan and whimper and plea. Felt the ghost of every time they'd been together nibbling at his skin.

"Can I...?" Michael wrapped his fingers around Victor's throat. Victor's eyes were half-lidded, dazed and yielding. He nodded, and Michael squeezed.

Victor was exquisite like this. Breathless beneath him. Covered in blood. Entirely, completely his. He came first, eyes shut, gasping when Michael let him breathe. His back curled off the bed and Michael met him with a firm kiss, pushing him down again, hips rocking faster, desperate and hungry for release of his own.

"Touch me," Michael said. Victor reached between them and squeezed the base of Michael's flushed cock. "Please," he whimpered, hips stuttering, breath fractured and loud between soft cries. "Vic, c'mon—"

"I want you begging," Victor whispered.

"Please, fuck—please." He kissed Victor again. Harder. Deeper. But Victor didn't move. "I swear to fucking God, Victor, please touch me, *please.*" And finally, *finally*, after a small, satisfied smile, Victor obliged.

Michael's hand slipped from around Victor's neck and he clutched the sheet. A loud gasp cut through the room. Victor hissed, hips stuttering toward the bed as Michael's body tensed and his muscles squeezed tight. The pitchy moans spilling over his lips were muffled by another kiss. Victor touched him until Michael swatted him away, spent and too sensitive.

They stayed in bed for a long time. The candles remained unlit. Something creaked in the hall. Footsteps, maybe. Wind, probably. Michael was pliant and tempered in Victor's arms. He let Victor kiss him roughly. Winced when Victor bit the cut on his neck again and didn't push him away when he rolled them over and pressed Michael into the sheets.

The night lasted and lasted.

Michael forgot to be quiet. He was drunk on Victor's magic, insatiable and ravenous.

At one point, his wrists were tied to the bed frame. At another, Victor was inside him again, fucking him hard and fast, with fresh blood on his mouth and wickedness in his eyes.

*This is dangerous*, Michael thought. Dangerous and primal and irresistible.

This magic. Victor Lewellyn. Port Lewis. Allocer.

But Victor was looking down at him, breathing with him, wanting him, and Michael knew there was no going back.

"You belong in my world," Victor said. He pulled Michael's legs around his waist and kept them lifted. "Do you understand me?"

He nodded. His shoulders rested on the bed, arms above his head, hands limp where they were tied to the bars of the wooden frame.

"Say it."

Michael Gates was reckless and promiscuous. He was lonely and guarded and made sure to stay unlovable. Until right then, in Victor's bed, with blood on his lips and magic in his veins.

"I belong with you," Michael said.

# Part Six: Party Crashers

MICHAEL WOKE WITH the night before clinging to his skin.

His throat was dry, limbs heavy and foreign. He hadn't felt like this in a while. Hangovers were one thing but coming down was another. Dark magic lingered the same way ecstasy did, souring his stomach and filling his head with cotton.

"Shit," he groaned. Nausea rolled through him. He stayed still and let it pass, eyes closed, enduring a headache that started behind his eyes and ended in his kneecaps.

Someone banged around in the kitchen downstairs. He turned onto his side to avoid the noise and came face to face with all eight of Elizabeth's legs. She sat on the edge of the bed, pink toes twitching on the white comforter, and didn't move an inch when Michael startled. He jerked away. It felt like all the blood in his head followed, sloshing back and forth.

His breath left him in an annoyed sigh.

*Last night.* He closed his eyes and remembered Victor underneath him. Eager, wet kisses. He touched two fingers to his wrist. Being restrained. Allowing Victor to use him, to take him apart completely, to squeeze every drop of resistance from him.

Michael swallowed hard. He hadn't done *that* in a while either. Rough, violent marathon sex had been reserved for hostels and raves until last night. He rolled onto his back and stared at the ceiling.

Victor had clamped his hand over the back of Michael's neck and held him down. *Don't come until I tell you to.* He'd spelled praises into his skin with teeth and claws. Called him beautiful. Turned Michael into a wrecked, boneless mess. They'd ended the night how they'd started it, though, with Michael in his lap, face to face, slow and gentle.

"Lizzy, your witch fucks like a porn star. Did you know that?" Michael glanced at the tarantula. She hadn't moved an inch. "Well, now you do."

He huffed and turned his gaze back to the ceiling. The room was empty. One of the blankets had been kicked to the ground and their clothes were strewn on either side of the bed. Seeing blood on the pillow and the sheets and the comforter, red and bright in the daylight, made his breath catch.

Somehow, he'd been maneuvered into boxers before they fell asleep. Blood was still crusted under his fingernails, but the rest had been wiped away. Bruises littered his hips and thighs and darkened his ribcage. Sitting up was painful. The room spun, tilting and whirling like a carnival ride.

Victor's voice came from beside the bookshelf. "You're awake."

"Yeah, and I might throw up on your spider if you don't move her."

"Here." His voice was suddenly closer. The bed dipped and a warm palm settled on Michael's shoulder. "Coffee."

The smell was enticing but made his stomach churn. "Not helping."

"It will," Victor assured him.

He leaned his forehead on Victor's shoulder and reluctantly took the coffee. He still hadn't opened his eyes, just let Victor guide the mug into his hands. "Is this how it always is?"

"Which part? The way you feel right now or the way you felt last night?"

Michael cracked his eyes open and looked at Victor. He was dressed in a plain T-shirt and black pants, clean and polished like always. "Both, I guess."

"Blood magic never loses its edge, but it can be easier to control and direct with practice."

"And the comedown?"

"I'm pretty sure you feel like shit because you've never been around magic before. Your body doesn't know what to do with it."

"Purge. That's what my body wants to do with it." He sipped his coffee and forced it to stay down.

"Magic is energy based. Wouldn't help much."

"Tell that to my stomach." Michael took a longer sip, easier than the last. Claws tickled his knuckles. "You okay?"

Victor hesitated. His brows furrowed and his lips thinned. "You used your safe word instead of commanding me last night." The statement came out stunted—nervous. There wasn't necessarily a question attached to it, but Michael assumed it was meant to be one.

"It worked," he said.

"I'm sorry I didn't notice your cues. I should've."

"You didn't hurt me. I mean, you did. A little. Sort of." Michael let out a frustrated breath and set the mug against his mouth to buy time. "That wasn't why I said it. You didn't do anything wrong."

"It's my responsibility to make sure you're comfortable."

"Christian threw me," Michael said. He met Victor's gaze. "Vassa did too. You warned me, but I didn't expect it and that's on me. It was a lot to handle all at once." Victor's face was soft under his palm. He scooted closer, ignoring the ache in his lower back that insisted he stay still, and pressed his lips to Victor's temple, the curve of his horn, his cheek. "You gave me everything I wanted." *And more.*

Victor's shoulders relaxed. He rested his hand over Michael's on his cheek. "You're such an anomaly, you know that?"

Michael's brows furrowed, smile small and curious. "Because I trusted you?"

"Because you didn't question me."

He snorted a laugh. "You expected me to?"

"Yeah, I did." Victor pulled Michael's hand to his mouth and kissed the red, raised mark circling his wrist.

Heat unfurled in his cheeks. Michael remembered Victor's voice. *You belong in my world.* The hard snap of his hips. How Victor had flipped him over and yanked him to his knees, mouth close to his ear, breathing hard. *Say it again.*

And Michael had. *I belong with you.* He'd said it over and over.

They watched each other, silent, before Michael kissed him on the mouth, slow and long. He needed a shower. He needed to eat something, even if he didn't want to, and he needed to get off his ass before his back got used to the idea of staying stationary.

"Is my sister still here?"

Victor shook his head. "She left a few minutes ago. Corey's been gone for a while."

"You ready for the party tonight?"

"The party I have to stay hidden in my room for? No, not really."

"You could always glamour yourself," Michael said. He grinned against Victor's lips. "Let me show you off. We'll drink good beer together, make small talk with Corey's friends."

A hummed, raspy laugh bubbled in Victor's throat. "I'm sure that'll go over well."

Thoughts of last night fell by the wayside. Michael kept the memories close—Victor's eyes on him as the night faded and turned from black to navy through the window, his arms tight around Michael's back, holding him close as they moved slowly, dreamily against each other. He kissed Victor again and relived the way it felt to be tender with the same person who had pushed him to carnal limits.

When Michael rallied the courage to stand, he was met with instant soreness. The night ached in him. His joints were creaky, hips tense and vertebrae tight. In the shower, his cuts burned. He noticed how the water was tinted translucent pink by his feet from blood left over on places he couldn't see, and when he looked in the mirror, he saw marks he hadn't noticed before. Fingerprints on his nape where Victor had held him down. Wide, dark bruises on his hips. Hickeys on his inner thighs and on his belly and red streaks from Victor's nails on the top of his ass. He looked at himself for a long time. Claimed. Empowered. Unbroken. He smiled at himself for a long time too.

The shower and a two-hour yoga session chased away most of the discomfort. Michael stretched on his mat, poised and focused, while his phone played indie music from the portable speaker, and Victor studied him quietly from the balcony.

Victor didn't say anything—just watched. And Michael allowed it, smiling smugly as he eased his ankle over the curve of his lower back.

JANICE: *Who was busy blowing your back out last night?*
MICHAEL: *r u d e*
JANICE: *I'm surprised you didn't wake up the neighbors.*
MICHAEL: *my bad*
JANICE: *Seriously who is it?*
MICHAEL: *I already told you it's the ghost*
JANICE: *Is he coming to the party?*

Michael smirked at his phone.

MICHAEL: *probably not. when will you be home?*
JANICE: *Grabbing booze & party favors with Corey. Twenty minutes.*

The moon hung low on the horizon. Constellations blinked awake. Fog hugged mossy tree trunks and snaked through branches. Michael ran his hand over the freshly shaved side of his head, flicking his gaze across his reflection. He remembered when his nostrils were decorated with silver studs. When the tattoo on his neck wasn't obscured by a Band-Aid and covered by a beige scarf.

"Fuck it," he mumbled and grabbed the matching silver studs from his jewelry dish. He pushed them into each nostril—the left side gave him trouble, but he winced and popped it through the almost-healed cartilage anyway—and adjusted the dainty silver chain that connected the two, curved over the tip of his nose. He sniffled, scrunching his nose until the urge to sneeze passed.

It'd been a long time since he'd worn jewelry. He slid a chunky hand-hammered silver ring onto his middle finger. A spiked ring onto his index. His shirt was crisp white, a stark contrast to his black jeans. A gray beanie slouched on the back of his head.

Victor's laughter appeared before he did. "You look like a Warped Tour poster."

"And you look like a Slayer album cover. Neither of us is winning here."

Another honest laugh boomed through the bathroom. Victor pressed his face into Michael's neck, hands settled on his waist, and caught his gaze in the mirror. "I'm kidding. You look great."

"I'm *not* kidding, but that doesn't mean you don't look great too," Michael said and flashed a grin.

Victor scoffed. He pressed a quick kiss to Michael's cheek, fingertip light as he traced the thin chain on his nose. "Any other secret piercings?"

He shook his head. "You?"

"I almost split my tongue when I was seventeen," Victor confessed. "But I chickened out at the last second."

"I've heard those are useful for a few things." His grin widened as he watched their reflections with playful eyes.

"Is that right?" Victor kissed his cheek again, the hinge of his jaw, nipped his pulse. "Care to elaborate?"

"It's not like you need a boost in that department—"

The front door opened. Janice's voice careened through the house. Her heels thudded on the wood floors and glasses clanked inside paper bags. Michael's grin faded. He sighed, enjoying the way Victor squeezed his hips.

"I'll sneak up here later," Michael whispered.

Victor nodded. He kissed him on the cheek again, tilted his head further and hummed when Michael turned to catch his lips. He was gone before the kiss ended. Black tendrils tickled Michael's lips and he licked it away, absently wondering if pieces of Victor lived in the smoke he left behind when he manifested and disintegrated.

"Michael! You home?" Janice called.

He gave his reflection another once-over and walked downstairs. Handles of liquor crowded the kitchen table. Corey shoved beer bottles into the fridge. A foam cooler lounged beside it, stocked with ice and cans.

Janice stacked red cups on the counter. She glanced at Michael and narrowed her eyes. "You put your nose rings back in."

"You're observant."

"You haven't worn 'em since before you left for Europe, huh?"

He shrugged dismissively. "Yeah, it was somewhere around then. When's everyone gonna be here?"

Corey closed the fridge. "A couple people are on their way now. I'm sure everyone else will trickle in as the night goes on." His eyes were fleeting as they swept over Michael. His ears turned pink, his throat bobbed, and he looked away. "What's your drink?"

"Tequila," Michael said. "Or beer. Anything, honestly."

"Should we start this off with shots then?" He glanced at Janice and lifted his brows, then looked at Michael. Janice whooped her approval. Michael wasn't sure what to make of Corey's pointed gaze until he grabbed a lime slice from a tray next to the red cups and rubbed it across the hollow of his thumb. "What're we toasting to?"

Janice held up her shot glass. "New beginnings."

Michael salted his hand and took the shot when it was handed to him. "Spontaneous connection."

Corey smiled at that—his perfect fucking smile—and said, "New friends." He tipped the shot glass against his lips and hissed once it was gone, gaze pinned to Michael as he bit into the lime and licked the salt from his thumb.

If Janice had heard Michael and Victor, Corey must've too. But still, he hadn't dialed back the flirting. Hadn't distanced himself. Hadn't asked. His persistence was worse after last night, somehow.

Michael tossed the shot back. Tequila burned his throat. He looked from Corey to Janice and exhaled sharply. "Guess it's time to turn the music on," he said, brows raised, excitement revving inside him.

A knock sounded at the front door. Corey's grin widened and he nodded. "Guess so."

MICHAEL HADN'T BEEN to a house party in a while. He'd almost forgotten how they worked. Walk. Talk. Lean against a wall. People watch. Pretend to look busy drinking. Smoke. He'd definitely forgotten how crowded they tended to be.

People sat on the couch, in laps, on the floor, perched on the kitchen counter. A group talked among themselves in the backyard. Music blasted from Corey's mobile speakers set in the corner of the living room. The entryway was crowded with bodies. People laughed and shrieked. Superstition slipped into almost every conversation Michael eavesdropped on.

*This is a Lewellyn house,* one girl said. *The cops won't come here.*

*Haunted I bet,* someone else said. *It's creepy as all hell.*

*I heard Corey scored some Essence. Think he'd sell any?*

"Essence," Michael parroted, sounding out the word carefully. He stood with his foot propped against the wall, leaning against the banister at the bottom of the stairs. The person who said it whipped toward him, eyes narrowed suspiciously. Michael's smile thinned. "What's that?"

"Who're you?" One of the girls wore a denim jacket over brightly patterned pants.

"Michael Gates. He, him. I'm Corey's roommate."

"Oh." Her lips quirked knowingly and she shot quick glances to the two people standing with her. They were an attractive group. Unapologetic and unassuming, just like Corey.

The one who'd spoken first regarded him with a lazy smirk. "If you haven't heard of Essence then you haven't been in Port Lewis very long."

Michael noticed how no one else introduced themselves. He arched a brow and stayed quiet.

"It's a drug, honey," they said. Their eyes were deep brown, only a shade or two darker than their skin. "Imagine if MDMA had a baby with cocaine and hit you like heroin."

"Sounds like a good time," Michael said.

"It is." They extended their hand. "Freddie. They. This is Marie and Leelah."

"She, her for both of us," said Leelah, the girl in the denim jacket.

"You're Corey's friends?" Michael sipped his beer.

"Yeah, we grew up together. You're from Arizona, right?" Freddie waited for Michael to nod. "No wonder Corey's been vague about you."

Michael tilted his head. "Vague?"

"You look like the kind of guy he'd chase." They dragged their eyes from his face to his ratty shoes. "And one he wouldn't share."

A breathy sigh came from behind Freddie. Then an irritated laugh. "Told you," Corey said, and met Michael's gaze. He pushed his arm past Leelah and curled his finger through Michael's belt loop, tugging him away. "Rowdy."

"Oh, come on," Freddie howled.

Michael snorted a laugh and followed Corey into the living room, thankful for an easy escape away from his pretentious friends. "They sure came on strong," he said, tucking his mouth close to Corey's ear.

The music was loud. Hard-hitting, sensual electronica cut through the room, lit by cell phone screens and the outdoor light creeping through the slider. Bodies pressed close. People danced and moved. One couple was pinned in the corner by the fireplace, hidden by shadows.

"Freddie will pounce on anyone who looks at them for half a second," Corey said. His palm rested on Michael's lower back as they stepped into the kitchen. "How's your night going?"

"Good, I guess. I just don't know anyone."

"You know me." Corey smiled as they stood beside the counter. His blue long-sleeve was half-tucked into straight-legged jeans. Blond hair expertly groomed. Gray eyes bright and confident, even in the dark. He was still nervous. It showed in his twitchy hand, how he barely touched Michael's knuckles. In his hesitation, how he opened his mouth, closed it, opened it again.

Michael chewed on his bottom lip. "I'm seeing someone," he blurted. Tragically, Corey's hand dropped away. "It happened like, really fast. Really fucking fast. I wasn't expecting it and we just... We got to know each other really well in a really short amount of time." How many times had he said *really?* Michael let out a long breath, angry at himself for rambling. "It's new but really intense and I just... I don't think..."

"I'm guessing this *someone* was here last night?" Corey's smile softened. He didn't look sad, not quite. He seemed at ease, as if he'd expected this.

"Yeah, he was. I'm sorry about that, we'll be more respectful next time."

"And I'm guessing you're completely one-hundred percent monogamous and dedicated to this someone?"

"We haven't..." Michael narrowed his eyes. He cocked his head, taken off guard. "We haven't talked about that yet."

"You should," Corey said. He reached past Michael to grab a half-empty bottle of tequila and two shot glasses from the dishwasher. He poured them. Handed one to Michael. Met his eye, again, like *that*. Devastatingly sweet and handsome and still interested, apparently. "Can I still flirt with you?"

No one had ever asked him that. His brow furrowed and he took the shot glass. "Yeah, if you want to."

"Do you like flirting with me? Because if I've been reading this wrong, let me know—"

"I flirt with everyone," Michael said. "I mean—I don't—not *everyone*. But I don't wanna lead you on when I've got..." His eyes flew to the figure easing through the crowded entryway. His tongue tripped. He blinked, once, twice, a third time. "When I've got..." Michael swallowed hard.

Victor wore a crisp gray button-up shirt with a smooth collar and a thin black tie. His charcoal jeans matched polished combat boots and his dark hair was effortlessly styled. The horns curving over his head were gone, same with his claws. But his eyes were still gold—too gold. They glinted, spectral and eerie, glamoured to appear human. He ran his hand along Michael's shoulder and cupped the back of his neck.

"You must be Corey," Victor said. His lips curved into a smile. "I'm Victor."

Corey looked Victor up and down. His playful smile didn't fade. He took his shot and nodded, stifling a small laugh. "Yeah, I'm Corey. He, him, by the way."

"Sorry, yeah, he, him for me too." Victor glanced at Michael expectantly.

*This is what a fish feels like when it gets stuck on a line, isn't it?* He drained the shot glass, snatched a lime slice from the place next to them, and bit into it. "You made it," he said, voice rasped by the alcohol.

"Took your advice," Victor said. He plucked the shot glass from Michael's hand, filled it with tequila, and tossed it back. "Tequila with no salt? That's a crime."

Corey barked a laugh.

Michael snorted. "You'll deal." He pulled a cigarette pack from his back pocket and nodded toward the sliding glass door. "Anyone want one?"

"No thanks." Corey checked his phone and grinned. "A friend of mine just pulled up anyway and I owe him a bindle, so—" He finished with a shrug. "I'll catch up with you guys later. Let me know if you want a hit before I run out."

"A hit of what?" Michael asked. He remembered the word. *Essence.*

"Janice didn't tell you? I picked up some E. Not a lot, just enough for tonight."

He glanced at Victor as he inched toward the slider, then steered his attention back to Corey. "Sure, yeah, maybe. We'll catch you in a bit," Michael said. Corey was already walking toward the entryway, flicking two fingers over his shoulder as a goodbye.

Frigid air bit at his hands. Michael took the unoccupied corner where the house met the glass door and put his back there, breathing in, breathing out. He fumbled with the lighter. His hands shook, nervousness battling with curiosity. Victor curled his palms around either side of Michael's wrists and held them still.

"This is a bad idea," Michael said. The cigarette finally lit and he took a long drag. "I mean, a monumentally awful fucking idea."

"Calm down," Victor teased, laughing through it. "I did an actual glamour spell. It won't wear off until tomorrow unless I break it on my own terms."

"What does that mean?"

"It means I don't have to concentrate on casting every goddamn second."

"And you haven't thought to do this before?"

"I have to actually prepare the spell and it's not like we schedule our time together." Victor rested his palm on the wall, efficiently caging Michael in the corner. He leaned close, grin sinister and striking. "*And* it takes a lot of energy to pull it off. Besides, you know all you need to do is ask and I'll happily glamour my claws away."

Michael blushed furiously. "Yeah, and if you lose focus, I face the consequences."

"Let me know in advance and I'll cook up a spell."

This was terribly embarrassing. "Fine, great. I'll do that."

Victor took the cigarette and set it between his lips. Smoke leaked from his nostrils, eyes still locked with Michael's. He exhaled at their feet, blowing ashy plumes between them. "Corey's nice," he said softly and leaned closer, mouth dragging across his cheek.

"He asked me if we're exclusive," Michael said. He let Victor lift the cigarette to his lips and took a drag.

"Are we?"

"Do you want to be?"

Victor's dark brows twitched. His jaw tightened.

"Does the thought of me being with someone else bother you?" Michael tested.

"Yes." The answer was too quick. Too sharp. And Michael loved the way Victor bit the word at him, possessive and rigid. Victor's cheeks darkened and he licked his lips, feigning restraint. "Sorry, that was..." He shook his head and took another drag. "Yeah, it would bother me if you were with someone else and I wasn't there," he said, deliberately slow.

*And I wasn't there.*

Michael's lips parted. He played the words back again just to be sure he'd heard them correctly.

"Would it bother you?" Victor asked.

He nodded, head tilted back against the cold wall, and smothered the cigarette butt under his shoe. "It would bother me, yeah. Unless I was there, and it was a mutually agreed upon thing."

Victor watched him carefully. "No emotional investments," he offered.

"Agreed. You don't go down on anyone but me."

"Fine. They don't stay in either of our beds."

"Obviously," Michael said through a laugh.

"Does this mean we're sleeping with Corey? Is that what we just decided?" Victor's lips grazed his chin.

"It means we're putting it on the table."

"I'm…" Victor growled softly, an intimate, haunting sound. "I'm a naturally jealous person. I know that, and I—"

"I like it," Michael mumbled, lolling his head to the side. The two beers and two shots convinced him to be honest—more honest than he'd normally be. "I like how possessive you are."

"You can always tell me if you don't."

"I know that."

People smoked cigarettes and joints on the other side of the cement patio in front of the slider. Others laughed and hollered inside. But Michael didn't care. He was too busy kissing Victor, running his hands over his neck and resting them beneath his ears. He was too busy smiling against his lips and moaning quietly when Victor opened his mouth wide and sucked on his tongue.

The night was profoundly normal. Victor licked salt from Michael's neck after taking another shot. They drank beers and mingled, talked with partygoers neither one of them would remember, people-watched and let their eyes wander over each other. Janice was too drunk to hold a conversation with Victor for very long, but she did manage to tell him her little brother should be kept on a leash with a very tight collar. Victor had grinned and said *I'll consider it* and Michael had felt each syllable burn between his thighs.

At one point, Michael was loose and electrified, halfway between buzzed and drunk, and he pulled Victor into the overly crowded living room. The dancing that started hours ago had turned into bodies grinding together. Couples kissed messily against walls. Someone snorted something out of a glass vial while a girl mouthed wetly at their neck.

Everything slowed. Everything tilted.

The music was loud and Victor was with him, eyes blazing, mouth kiss-bitten, and Michael wanted everyone to know. He snarled at a couple to get off the couch—*this is my house, assholes, move*—and shoved Victor down.

"Technically it's *my* house," Victor said.

Michael could barely hear him. He slid into Victor's lap, thighs on either side of him, and rolled his hips. His body followed the music, back arched, grinding shamelessly against Victor in a room full of people. Power felt reckless and perfect like this. He tugged on Victor's tie, ran his fingertips across the buttons lining his torso, watched his pupils dilate and his teeth dive into his bottom lip. Bass rattled his lungs. The world narrowed down to Victor underneath him, his slack jaw and painful swallow, and the way his lashes fluttered when Michael ground down on him.

The song changed to something slower. Easier to dance to. Michael held onto Victor's shoulder and leaned back, eager for Victor's hand on him, under his shirt, skirting his chest. Hungry for Victor's grip on his hips to tighten to the point of pain, harder, *more*, until he gasped and flinched.

"Sorry, sweetheart," Victor said, snapping the words close to his ear. "But you're not making this easy."

*Sweetheart.* Michael grinned. "Making what easy?" He punctuated his question with another hard roll of his hips.

Victor's breath gusted his neck. He gripped Michael's ass and pulled him closer, teeth sudden and stinging over a hickey under his jaw. They were both too drunk to show much finesse. Their kisses were sloppy. Touches messy and fumbling. But it was good. It was so fucking good to be with someone again.

Someone who wanted him. Someone who liked being claimed in a room full of people, who pulled on Michael and kissed him deeply and laughed with him.

A person on the floor snorted powder from another vial and cursed under their breath. *Fuck, this is good shit.*

Michael didn't listen. He was too busy holding on to the back of Victor's head and hoping no one noticed Victor's palm between his legs, rubbing him through his jeans. He caught a few insignificant words. *Overdose. Careful. Don't do too much.*

"Upstairs," Michael blurted, panting against Victor's ear as he teased at his zipper.

They stumbled through the entryway. The staircase was crowded with people, but they weaved through them easily. Victor mouthed at the back of his neck. The room wasn't spinning, but the walls pulsed and everything moved and he'd probably fall if it weren't for Victor keeping him steady. Two girls kissed at the top of the stairs, hands under skirts and over bras.

The moment there wasn't anyone in front of them, Victor reached around and palmed him through his jeans again. Michael shot out a hand to catch himself on the wall, laughing when Victor stumbled into him, grinning against his neck.

A door opened. Corey stepped from his bedroom, head tipped back, pinching his nose with two fingers. He sniffled and glanced at them, eyes glazed, mouth curved into a timid smile. "Where are you two going?" he asked, suggestion and playfulness thick in his voice.

Michael didn't know what to do or say. His heart raced. He waited for Victor's lips to touch his ear, for his raspy, low whisper. *Well?*

"You wanna come?" Michael asked. He met Corey's gaze and bit his lip, trying not to make a sound as Victor's teeth sank into his neck again.

Corey's mouth fell open. Shock came first, then disbelief, and finally a stuttered question. "You're... Are you—I mean, really? Seriously?"

Michael loved this. He loved watching Corey blush. He loved how it seeped into his bones—this control, this raw, inelegant desire. "Serious as a train wreck," he said, fisted his hand in Corey's shirt, and hauled him into a kiss.

Corey's back hit the wall in the hallway. Michael pressed him against it, caged between Corey's strong chest and Victor's torso snug against his spine. His body was on fire, urgent and wound tight, desperate to touch and be touched. There were hands in his hair. Corey's hands. Fingers drifting under his shirt. Victor's fingers. Kissing Corey was worlds apart from kissing Victor. Corey kissed exactly how Michael had imagined he would—he followed every movement Michael made, nipping and licking whenever prompted to.

"We're..." Corey bared his neck and Michael didn't hesitate to bite him. "We're really doing this, huh? Yeah? Okay, yep... Wow." His hips stuttered against Michael's. "Holy shit, *wow*."

Victor muffled a laugh against Michael's nape. "Bedroom?"

They stumbled into Michael's room, hands and mouths on necks and shoulders. Michael had dreamed of a night like this for a long time. Being with someone like Victor, caring about him, wanting him, trusting him, and bringing in another partner for the night. Another mouth. Another voice. Another pair of hands. Another body to explore. Corey had a lovely mouth and a great voice. He had capable hands and an exquisite body.

Michael wanted Victor to see him with someone else and hold him down after. He wanted Victor to tell Corey what to do to him, to direct them, to command them. He wanted Victor to force them both to their knees and say *Michael's mine* while they were at his mercy. He wanted—

"Whoa, whoa, stop," Victor hissed. He pulled Michael from the edge of the bed. Yanked Corey by the back of his shirt just before he fell onto it. "Elizabeth, what the hell are you doing?"

Michael should've let Janice call an exterminator.

The tarantula stood on the bed with her front legs raised and her fangs extended. She lunged at them, hopping again and again, agitated and overly aggressive.

Corey gasped and stumbled back. He tried to grab Michael's wrist, but Michael pulled free. He heaved an irritated sigh. *Mood killer.* "It's fine," Michael said, turning his gaze to Corey. "Lizzy's his pet."

Lizzy jumped again, this time directly at Michael.

"Let's not call her a pet," Victor said through clenched teeth.

"I thought you tossed it over the fence?" Corey said. His wide eyes flicked from Michael to Victor then back to Michael.

Michael rolled his eyes. He was far too buzzed for this. "Yeah, well, she came back."

"This is fucked up, dude. Really fucked up. You guys do whatever you want, but—shit, seriously?" Corey turned to leave and stopped in his tracks. "A mouse too? We're infested!"

"What?" Michael followed his gaze.

There, standing on its back legs, little hands cleaning its snout, was a white mouse with round ears and beady red eyes. It didn't move, just stood there, unbothered.

"It's cute," Michael cooed and shot Corey a hard glare. "It probably wandered in from outside. Chill out."

"It didn't," Victor said, voice grave.

Shouts erupted downstairs. *What the hell? Watch out! How did a dog get in here?* People hollered. Things banged and glasses clinked. Something galloped on the stairs. Victor's sigh was enough to confirm that he knew what it was—*who* it was. His hand pressed to Michael's waist. "Stay behind me," Victor said.

Loud, deep growls came from outside the door. Sniffs from a busy nose. Scratches from big paws.

"Luna," Victor warned. "Don't—"

The bedroom door opened and a black dog leaped at them. She was lean and tall, a Doberman with rows of white teeth and pin-straight ears. Her snout curled back into a fierce snarl, body poised to lunge.

"Luna!" Victor shouted. He pushed on Michael's waist, guiding him backward. Corey had already scrambled away and was hugging the far wall next to the nightstand. "It's me, girl. Calm down."

A voice came from the hallway, faintly familiar, as if he'd heard it in another life, in a memory that wasn't his. "She doesn't recognize you," Vassa said. They stepped into the bedroom, face obscured by a dark hood, thin, petite build wrapped in black from head to toe. "Luna, enough."

The dog immediately went quiet.

"What the hell are you doing here?" Victor asked.

Vassa pulled the wide hood back. Their teal hair was striking against white skin, eyes crystalline blue. "I'm disappointed," they said, aiming the words at Victor. "You of all people? *You?*"

"Can you explain what exactly I did wrong before you start lecturing me?"

Their gaze shifted to Michael. An indignant snort followed, full mouth pressed into a thin line. Scars littered their neck and hands, the only flesh visible above their high-collar and the buttoned sleeves of their cloak. "You know, I was surprised when word-of-mouth led us here, but I'm not surprised to see you messing around with your buyers."

"Vassa!" Victor's voice deepened into howls and screams and hisses.

"You're slinging Essence, Victor! Thalia and Gerard have been hunting down dealers for months and the last big hit was tonight, here, in *your* house, at *your* party. How do you explain that?"

Victor's body went rigid. His face dropped, confusion mingling with something worse. Betrayal, maybe. Pain. He turned from Vassa to Michael and shook his head, brows knitted, mouth agape. "Do you have anything to do with this?"

Michael's pulse pounded in his ears. He gave a curt shake of his head, attempting to find a minuscule sense of the bravery he usually clung to in situations like these. Dangerous situations. Peculiar, nerve-racking, unsavory situations. "I overheard some people talking about it earlier, but no, I have no idea what it is."

"Who was talking about it?" Vassa bit out.

"Corey's friends." Michael stepped away from Victor, glancing between him and Vassa. "Apparently, Corey scored some for the party. Why the hell is it such a big deal?"

"Look, man. I got it from some girl at school, okay? I'll tell you whatever you want," Corey whined. He shuffled closer to the wall, eyes bulged and fearfully pinned to Luna.

Black, smoky tendrils snaked from beneath Vassa's heeled boots. "Give me her name."

"I don't even know her! It was… Shit, it was like Emily or Ariel or something. What the fuck…" Corey's frantic gaze shot from Luna to the black smoke twisting into vines around Vassa's legs. "What the hell are you?"

The air ran from them, as if it knew what Vassa was, what Victor was, what they'd done together, to each other, and a bone-deep cold settled in the room. Energy shifted, buckling inward like a kneecap forced from the socket.

The whites of Vassa's eyes darkened. Their pupils expanded until two obsidian pools stared out from beneath long lashes lined in dagger-sharp eyeliner. "I'm the thing under your bed," they taunted. "The thing in your closet. The thing you hoped a night-light would scare away."

"Vassa, c'mon, stop it," Victor hissed, as a parent would to a child.

Heels clicked the floorboards in the hallway. "Necromancers are *so* dramatic." Her voice chimed, jubilant and easy. She walked into the room without pause, her brunette hair styled into long ringlets and crowned with a crystal tiara. Jewels framed her doe eyes, freckles dusted her nose, and glitter was pressed to her cheeks. "Willow, get away from that spider before it eats you," she snapped.

"Tarantula," Victor corrected sternly.

"*Tarantula*," the girl sarcastically parroted.

Whoever this lost Urban Outfitters employee was, Michael wanted her gone. He wanted them all gone. Vassa. Corey. Even Victor. Just for a few minutes, just so he could catch his breath.

The white mouse—Willow—darted across the floor. She climbed the girl's knee-high socks, the lace stockings underneath, and disappeared into the pocket of her slouchy petal pink sweater-dress.

"I told you to stay in the hall and keep watch, Christy," Vassa said.

"Well, I don't happen to take orders from you, darkling. Besides, I think I can help with this situation, since, you know—" She pointed to her temple and forced a smile. "I'm psychic. Now, which one of you is Victor?"

Victor huffed. "I'm not the one you're after." He nodded at Corey. "He is."

"Fine, and what about..." Christy looked at Michael and tilted her head, staring at him intently. Her mauve lips pinched and she perched her slender hands on her hips. "Don't I know you?" When Michael shook his head, she gasped delightedly. "You're totally that travel blogger, huh? I follow you on Instagram." She shot out her hand, waited until he hesitantly grasped it, and shook. "I'm Christy Carroway."

Michael tried on a smile, but it was forced and small. "Michael Gates."

Something warm filtered through. Sunlight illuminated his thoughts and magic seeped into him, light as a feather, soft and gentle. Christy kept his hand in hers, eyes wide and unblinking, flicking around his face. He felt her sifting through thoughts. Feelings. Memories.

"Don't be scared," she whispered. Honesty came naturally to her, same with sweetness. She smoothed her thumb reassuringly over his knuckles. Michael accidentally thought of Victor. Probably because he couldn't help being afraid. Probably because Victor was the only piece of this strange new world he could count on. "Oh, dear," Christy said softly. "Your poor heart—"

Michael yanked his hand back and clutched it to his chest. "Is none of your business," he said.

"Sorry," she blurted and shook out her hands, her head, her hips. "Sometimes I can't help what I see." Her attention shifted to Victor and she swallowed hard, eyes fleeting and nervous as she looked from him to Corey. "Come here, honey."

Corey didn't move. He winced though, as if a thin blade had pierced his temple.

"She said *come here*," Vassa hissed. The black smoke dancing around their feet jolted through the air and latched around Corey's wrists, his ankles, and slid seductively up his chest.

Victor stepped in front of Michael again. His fingertips trembled when they landed on Michael's waist, easing him backward toward the balcony. "Take her," he said under his breath, mouth angled over his shoulder. Lizzy skittered onto Michael's shirt and climbed until she was settled on his shoulder. "Stay out there, all right?"

*No.* That was Michael's first reaction. He didn't want to leave Victor alone in his bedroom with the person who'd killed him—accident or not—and a psychic who had seen the inside of Michael's scars. He planted his feet and stayed.

"Vassa! This isn't how we're doing this," Christy shouted.

"Quiet, white witch," Vassa snapped back.

The air quaked. Night deepened into a vicious version of itself, turned inside out, rabid and ripped apart. Victor shed his glamour the same way a snake shed its skin. He slid from it, shaking layers away until his horns appeared, ringed in black wisps, and his prominent bones hollowed his skin, and claws tipped his fingers. Even his shadow ran from him, stretching and stretching, as if it might break away and take shelter somewhere else.

Magic like this, tangled and too powerful, made Michael nauseous.

"That's enough," Victor growled. He waved his hand and the black tendrils around Corey's wrists and ankles disintegrated. He vanished and reappeared before Vassa, so much taller, so much deadlier. "You're done." Even with the music playing in the living room and people still hollering on the stairs, his voice carried, louder, more animal than human.

The lights flickered. Michael's thoughts were soupy and drowned, too light, too distant. He swallowed the lump in his throat and squeezed his eyes shut, willing his stomach to stop churning and his mind to clear.

Vassa didn't back down, but their magic retreated. "I can feel his heartbeat on your skin," they whispered. "I can taste him inside you."

Michael leaned against the French door. He cracked his eyes open and they were all still there. Victor and Vassa, staring at each other. Christy with her fingers curled intimately around Corey's hand. Luna, the black dog with a mean bark, standing beside Vassa with her ears pinned and her teeth bared at Victor.

"Don't make me hurt you, Vassa," Victor said, a plea and a warning.

"I have it," Christy piped, rambling it again and again. "I have it, I've got it. He wasn't lying, it's some girl in his Psychology class. Esther."

Vassa's eyes turned blue again. They stepped back and Luna followed. "Where's the supplier?"

"He doesn't know. Esther said something about Venice, but that's it."

"Venice Beach?" Vassa's top lip curled.

"I have no idea. All I got was the word."

Vassa heaved an irritated sigh. "Fine. We'll let Gerard know."

"*You'll* let Gerard know," Christy corrected. "The only reason I'm here is because I owed Jordan a favor. You know that. Let's just get this over with so I can get out of here."

"Get what over with?" Victor asked.

"We can't leave them here with their memories intact," Vassa spat.

*Them.* Michael fumbled for the knob on the French door. Vassa glared at him but didn't make a move. Maybe because they were enjoying the fear that crossed his face. Probably because Victor's shadow suddenly filled the floor, and the lights flickered until they popped, and his voice rumbled like thunder. "He's mine, Vassa. Take what you want from Corey, but Michael won't be touched."

"Fine, fine," Christy said, exasperated. "Put your fangs away, both of you."

Vassa let out a sharp, threatening breath—a hiss but deeper.

"A year is all it took for you to conveniently forget who I am," Victor whispered. Bitterness lived with sadness, unfurling from him in waves. "You answer my texts, you make promises, but it's now, here, like this, when I finally see you again?"

Vassa's nostrils flared. Their shoulders pulled tight and their eyes softened, but they didn't move or breathe or say another word.

"Finish what you started and go," Victor said. He glanced at Christy and shook his head. "Careful who you run with, lightworker. Darklings and demons don't play well with witches like you."

Christy smirked. She stood in front of Corey, arms folded casually across her chest. "You have *no* idea who my circle-mates are, and honestly? I don't need you to tell me to be careful, because they don't scare me." She pointed at Vassa. "And you don't scare me." She jabbed her index finger at Victor. "Not even with your horns on."

Michael couldn't help it, he laughed. What else was he supposed to do? It was a sharp, childish, exhausted laugh, the kind inspired by alcohol and sleeplessness. "I like you," he said, and raised his brows at Christy, then turned to look at Victor. "I like her."

"Go outside," Victor said through a sigh. He gestured to Vassa, Christy, and Corey—who looked absolutely terrified—with a twirl of his hand. "Clean this shit up. Make sure he doesn't remember anything."

"Don't worry. It'll be like he blacked out," Christy assured.

Victor looked at Vassa one last time, then reached past Michael, opened the door and pushed him onto the balcony.

LATE-NIGHT AIR cooled Michael's hot cheeks. He took a deep breath, thoughts still tripping over what he'd witnessed. He had his back turned to the twin doors leading to his bedroom, but Christy's whispered voice and Luna's steady panting fluttered onto the balcony with him anyway.

"You're used to this," he said. Elizabeth walked into his palm when he held his hand out to her, numbed by the alcohol coursing through his veins, and too tired and drunk to be afraid of her. "And I'm definitely not."

"I didn't expect this to happen," Victor said. He kept his distance, straight-backed and utterly still, standing between Michael and the French doors. "Are you okay?"

"Probably not."

"Is there anything I can do to make you feel better?"

"You can tell me what Essence is. That'd be a good place to start."

Corey gasped from inside. Christy's voice got louder—*you're okay, you're all right.* Even out here, with the fresh air and the moon high above him, Michael couldn't shake the magic crawling under his nails, snaking over his bones, curling around his throat. He absolutely did not want to throw up, so he plopped on his rear and closed his eyes.

Victor was beside him in two steps, hand warm on his shoulder. "Michael—"

"Essence," he choked out, then held his breath. Elizabeth's prickly toes danced gently on his palm. "Go. Tell me."

He hesitated, but after shifting from foot to foot and letting out a short sigh, Victor gave in. "How you feel right now? The surge of power that comes from being around magic? That's because the air is saturated in energy. It gets trapped in water, smoke, sage leaves, ashes—it can be harvested that way. Bottled and powdered. People wanna feel the same way we did last night, so they get high off the residue spells and rituals leave behind."

"Not everything I felt last night had to do with magic," Michael said.

Victor paused at that. He held his breath, considering, but let the comment slide. "What I'm saying is that dark magic—addictive magic—is the most sought after to be transmuted into Essence. It's the most powerful. The most potent."

"And humans buy it?"

"Sometimes other witches too."

"And Vassa thought you were the one creating and selling it? That's why they stormed into our house with their dog and the psychic?"

"Yeah. That's exactly why."

"Awesome, great. Wonderful. If Essence is such a taboo thing, then why didn't you fucking say anything when Corey offered us some?"

"I assumed he meant Ecstasy, I didn't think anyone would be stupid enough to bring Essence to a Lewellyn house," Victor said. He sucked air through his teeth and huffed.

Before Michael could ask another question, the door opened. A wave of thick, hot magic swept from the bedroom and stuck to his skin. Head-spinning, intoxicating, and enough to make him turn away, face tucked close to his arm.

Vassa's voice cut through, as bitter as the cold. "It's done. He's passed out."

"Goodnight, Vassa." Victor stitched threats into simple phrases, and that one was easy to recognize. *Goodnight* was interchangeable with *get out*.

Heels clicked on the wood floors. Christy's voice was hushed and shy. *Is he all right?* And Vassa's clipped response sounded distant, as if they'd stepped into the hall. *Let's go.* Paws followed. People downstairs chattered restlessly as the two witches left the house.

Michael was definitely going to get sick. Especially after Victor opened both French doors and shooed the magic out as if it were pollen. He placed Elizabeth on the balcony wall beside a potted succulent and brushed past Victor, eyes trailing Corey's sleeping form draped awkwardly in his bed. He slammed the bathroom door behind him, locked it, and barely made it to his knees before he was heaving tequila and beer and whatever else was in his stomach into the toilet.

Throwing up sucked. It always did. But it was worse this time, somehow. Probably because magic was the cause, coupled with too much booze and too much of everything else the night before. Michael needed to sleep for two days. He needed to think about his life, where it was going, what he'd allowed it to become.

Thankfully, Victor didn't manifest in the bathroom with him. Michael took out his jewelry, washed his face, brushed his teeth, flossed, moisturized, brushed his teeth again, and stared at his glassy, red eyes looking back at him from the mirror.

"Get on your laptop," he whispered to himself. "Book a one-way ticket to Thailand. Don't look back."

That would be the best decision. The safest choice.

Michael rolled his bottom lip between his teeth.

He knew it wasn't an option, though. Not this time.

The party was still in full swing. When he opened the door and crept into the hallway, people were seated on the stairs and dancing in the living room and shotgunning beers in the kitchen, but he had no intention of joining them. Instead, he trailed his hand along the wall to stay steady, counted the four steps leading to the attic, and walked into Victor's bedroom.

# Part Seven: Blood Stains

MICHAEL BARELY REMEMBERED falling asleep. He'd crawled into Victor's bed, hadn't said a word, closed his eyes and that was it. He didn't know what time it was. The sun was high in the sky and his phone was probably still in the pocket of his jeans that were crumpled on the floor. The house was silent and he was alone.

Food sounded unpleasant but necessary. His mouth was stale, eyes achy and head still tilting back and forth. Okay, so, alcohol and magic? Hard no. Memories filtered through. Vassa and Christy. Giving Victor a messy lap dance on the couch. Michael closed his eyes and groaned. *How embarrassing.* Shots and beers and cigarettes. Almost dragging Corey into a threesome might've been the worst and best decision Michael had made all night. He was grateful Corey wouldn't remember it.

"Fuck," he muttered. Hangovers were inconvenient and uncomfortable. He wished the cures really worked—a green juice or a shot or greasy food. But they never did. "Vic?"

No shadows moved.

"Victor?"

A second passed before the air shifted and Victor appeared, dressed in a plain black shirt and brown pants. He leaned against the door, quiet and watchful, with his hands in his pockets.

"Hey," Michael tested.

Gold eyes drifted to the floor. "How're you feeling?"

"Like I've been wasted for two nights in a row. Sorry for—" Michael rolled his eyes and scrubbed a hand over his face. "—*everything*."

"What do you mean?" Victor tilted his head, confused.

"Was the sloppy lap dance a nightmare or did it really happen?"

"Oh, no, that happened. That definitely happened."

Michael groaned again.

"I don't remember complaining though."

"And me *attacking* Corey, Jesus Christ." He covered his face with his hands. "Yeah, all that stuff." He circled one finger in the air. "That's what I'm sorry for."

The bed dipped under Victor's weight. "That dance wasn't sloppy," he said. Michael heard the presence of a smile on his face. "It was sexy. *You* were sexy—"

A sharp laugh punched from him. "Fuck off, oh my God."

"I wouldn't lie to you," Victor purred. He slid his palm across Michael's bare stomach. "Your sister's making breakfast, by the way. Waffles, I think."

He didn't know the protocol for Vassa. If he should bring them up or not. If he should ask whether Victor intended to see them again. What Victor had meant, exactly, when he'd told Vassa that Michael was his.

"Yeah, okay." He trailed his fingertips over Victor's knuckles. Questions formed and deconstructed on his tongue, clumsy like his thoughts, muddied and disjointed. He kept them to himself and swung his legs off the bed. "Do you want some?"

"I don't think my glamour would hold for very long after..." Victor fiddled with his thumbs, claws tapping again and again. "I just—I drank *and* casted last night, and Vassa's behavior didn't help keep my temper in check, so." He shrugged, offering a weak smile. "I don't wanna stretch myself thin."

"Are you out of mana, Victor?" Michael teased, which earned him a playful swat to the side of his hip. "I'm kidding, I get it."

"I don't need to give Allocer's demonic energy another reason to influence my body any more than it already has," he added quietly, flicking his eyes up toward his horns then to his big, clawed hands.

"Yeah, you were..." Michael trailed off. Frightening? Powerful? Different? "You were pissed," he said softly. "I haven't seen anything like that before."

Victor was quiet for a long time. He kept his hand curled over Michael's thigh, gaze flicking from the bed to the window. The wrongness that had filled the room last night and tickled his skin when he'd first moved in seemed nonexistent. Even like this, hungover and bruised in the aftermath of Victor's terrible, haunting voice and his unbelievable magic, Michael felt safe.

"Are you afraid of me?" Victor asked. He sounded unlike himself in a way that pulled hard on Michael's heartstrings. Helpless. Wilted and weak and ashamed. His wide eyes found Michael's gaze again and stayed there, trapped and wounded.

That was the problem, wasn't it? In the beginning, Michael had been far too curious about Victor to be scared of him, and now he cared far too much for Victor to be afraid of him. He closed the space between them and pressed their foreheads together.

"I should be," he whispered. "But no, I wasn't afraid of you last night and I'm not afraid of you today and I probably won't be afraid of you tomorrow."

Victor's shoulders relaxed and he sighed, breath warm on Michael's mouth.

Janice called from downstairs. "Hey, dipshits! I made food!"

"Go eat." Victor's lips brushed the bridge of his nose and landed on his cheek, a chaste, sweet kiss.

Michael tugged his jeans on and took a sweatshirt Victor handed him. The fabric smelled like old cologne and cookies. He tugged it on, giddy to have something of Victor's. Something simple. Something entirely human and *his*.

Before he opened the bedroom door, Victor's lips grazed his ear, hands light on his hips. "So," he hummed, rasped and playful, "if I make a playlist—"

"Fuck you," Michael said through a laugh and shrugged him away.

A LARGE PLATE crowded with fluffy waffles sat on the counter next to a tub of butter. Janice hadn't waited for them. She forked another waffle onto her plate just as Michael stepped into the kitchen.

"Syrup." She pointed at the syrup bottle with her fork, then jabbed it at a pink pitcher. "Juice."

"You only cook after getting laid. Spill."

"That isn't true," Janice spat.

Michael drenched two waffles in syrup. "Was it Coffee Guy?"

Janice snorted.

"It was, huh?"

She stopped chewing and glared at the ceiling. "He moans like a zebra," she said and shoved another bite in her mouth.

Michael set his plate down to properly laugh. It was full-bodied laughter, the kind that made his head hurt worse and his eyes water. "He moans like a zebra," he mocked, letting another bout of laughter shake through him. "*A zebra?*"

She tried not to laugh but eventually caved. "I swear to God, he does. It was some Lion King shit, Michael. I'm not even—"

He howled at her, laughter loud and bright. *This is surreal*, he thought. Last night he'd watched a necromancer restrain his roommate with black smoke, and this morning he was laughing with his sister as he would on any other morning, after any other party, in any other house.

"Screw you, stop it," she said, giggling with her mouth full. "Did you have fun with Victor?"

"Yeah, we had a good time." He wiped his eyes with the heel of his palm. "You like him?"

"He seems cool. Didn't you guys, like, *just* meet though?"

"We've gotten to know each other kinda fast, I guess. It's new and it's intense, but it works."

Janice nodded. He knew that look—brows knitted, eyes downcast, pushing food around her plate.

"Say it and get it out of the way," Michael snapped.

"He's not married, right?"

"*No.*"

"Okay, good." She filled a glass with orange juice and pushed it toward him. "Sorry, but—" A short shrug. A thin, bitter smile. "—*married* is your type, so."

"You ever gonna let me get over that? Or is this my punishment for sleeping with your boyfriend?"

Janice tilted her head one way then the other, deliberating. "You deserve it."

"I loved him, Janice," Michael said. Maybe the hangover had convinced him to be honest. Maybe it was Victor or the devastating magic he'd witnessed last night. Maybe Michael was tired of hiding his hurt behind a callous exterior. Janice stopped chewing and shot him a wilted look. "I did. I know it was stupid—*I* was stupid and naïve and selfish, but a part of me thought he'd pick me in the end. That's how it always goes, right? An older guy has someone younger and desperate on the side who'll do whatever he wants, right? Who'll cover bruises with makeup and doesn't mind getting called a whore because one day he'll get the ring, right?" Janice hadn't blinked or moved. "*Right?*"

"Michael, I didn't—"

"You didn't know because I was still the slutty little brother who slept with your boyfriend."

"That isn't fair," she bit out.

Michael forked two more waffles onto his plate and shook his head. He walked away, tossing their father's famous words over his shoulder as he went. "Life's not fair."

"Michael!" Janice's voice came out shrill and wobbly. She didn't follow him.

Corey walked down the stairs as Michael walked up them. He stopped in place, watching Michael skeptically. A dark blush painted his cheeks and he pawed restlessly at a crescent bruise on his throat—marks from Michael's teeth.

"Everything okay?" Corey asked, glancing down the stairs then back to Michael.

"Yeah, it's just family stuff. Don't worry about it."

"I, uh... I woke up in your..." He rubbed the back of his neck. "I woke up in your bed. Did we...?"

"You passed out while I was smoking a cigarette with Victor. Someone dared us to kiss and we did, but that was it." The lie tasted sterile, but the relief on Corey's face made him feel better about telling it. "We didn't sleep together or anything, don't worry."

Corey smiled sheepishly. "I'm eighty percent sure I blacked out and can't remember something *really* important."

"Like us having sex?" Michael listed his head, smile coy and loose.

"Yes, exactly like that."

"Nothing happened," Michael assured. "Like I said, we kissed. That's it."

"Was it a good kiss?"

He cringed. "Messy, actually. We weren't exactly on our game last night."

Corey mirrored a cringe back at him.

"Which is probably a good thing, right?" Michael blurted. "We're roommates. We probably shouldn't..." He rolled his eyes and forced a clenched grin. "Compromise that, you know?"

Essence had changed the way Michael felt about sleeping with Corey. Especially when Victor would be involved. Despite how fun Corey might be, having him in their bed didn't seem worth it now. Not after he knew what Essence was. How it was harvested. What might happen if Corey tasted magic on them and told the wrong people.

"Oh, of course, yeah. You're totally right. We'd be a mess and you've got your new guy now and..." Corey's voice faltered, slipping into disappointment. "I get it."

Michael's first instinct was to apologize. He opened his mouth, but the words stayed locked away. *I'm sorry. I don't know if I can trust you. It was actually a really good kiss.* Some things were better left unsaid, he thought. Because no matter how perfect Corey's teeth were and how handsome he happened to be, Michael already belonged to someone else.

"Thanks for letting me crash in your bed," Corey added. He flashed another somber smile and bounced down the stairs.

*At least that's over.* Michael inhaled a deep breath through his nose. He should've stopped flirting with Corey the moment he'd seen Victor. He should've known better. He shouldn't have risked a potential friendship over the allure of possibility. But he'd been here before. Gone through this cycle before. Slept with friends who became *friends* and lost them to jealousy or awkwardness weeks later.

Michael hadn't screwed it up *too* bad. A friendship with Corey was still salvageable.

His relationship with Janice? That was something else entirely.

The attic door cracked open and a single golden eye peeked at him from inside. "Did you bring me waffles?" Victor whispered.

Michael smirked. He crossed the hallway and stepped into the attic, welcomed by Victor's lips on his temple and his warm body and a quiet purred, "You *did*. Thank you, babe."

THE NEXT WEEK passed in increments of avoidance.

Michael dodged Janice each morning, waiting until she'd left for class or work to go downstairs for coffee. His days were spent researching places in Port Lewis to blog about and scrolling through pictures he'd taken in Europe, crawling into Victor's bed after breakfast and cooking together in the late afternoons. When Michael wasn't responding to an e-mail or staging his ring light for a selfie, he was enjoying the empty house by fucking Victor in every possible place he could.

The balcony? Twice.

Staircase? His back was still sore from that.

Kitchen? Never on the table—always against the counter.

Obviously, Janice's room was off limits. Same with Corey's.

They'd almost been caught once, but just once. Two days ago, on Wednesday, Victor had pinned Michael to the door in the laundry room which was positioned across from the kitchen in the entryway. His pants had been pushed down, shirt rucked up, and Victor had whispered terrible, wonderful things as he touched him, pressing his cheek to the smooth, cool door, telling him to arch his back—*good*—to keep his hands on the door too—*like that*—and fingered him fast and dirty. When Janice came home, she'd tossed her keys on the counter. Michael had held his breath, desperately hoping Victor would pity him enough to stop. He hadn't. Victor had been relentless, his long, bony fingers thrusting hard and deep, rubbing and curling and massaging, until Michael had gasped and squirmed, eyes watering, body quivering.

"Michael, are you home?" she'd called.

Victor had worked Michael through a white-hot orgasm, smothering the sound of his heaved breaths with a clawed hand curled around his mouth. Janice's shadow had crossed the bottom of the door and Victor had vanished while Michael was trying to catch his breath, successfully stealing her attention by opening a door upstairs.

"Okay, whatever," Janice had hollered. "Can't ignore me forever, though."

Janice had turned on the TV and Michael had crept to his room. Victor's smug smile had been wiped away by Michael's wet mouth and loose jaw and the tight grip he kept on the base of Victor's cock, edging him until he gripped Michael's shoulder and said *please.*

The time he spent with Victor in that old, creaky house sometimes felt playful and sometimes felt raw, as if he'd been cracked open wide and spilled over the floor, all his secrets and insecurities and mistakes laid out like a tarot spread. Future. Past. Present. Sometimes Michael grinned around the filter of a post-sex cigarette as they stood together on the balcony, wearing hickeys and blood like badges. Other times he curled into Victor's chest, shaking and wet-cheeked, and hoped Victor didn't see him as broken for needing to be held.

It was Friday morning. The sun peeked through trees and chased away the witching hours to reveal a navy sky. Victor had trailed his lips down Michael's body, touched him reverently, slowly, and smothered his careless sounds with deep, unhurried kisses. As Michael caught his breath, he felt a knuckle curl under his damp lashes.

"Will you ever tell me?" Victor asked, rubbing tears between his fingers.

Michael kept his gaze on the forest, illuminated by a soft, sleepy sun, on the other side of the French doors. "You fuck me like you love me," he said because it was the truth and he didn't have room for much else anymore. Not with Victor, at least. He turned to look at him, at his black horns and fine mouth, at his fiery eyes and copper skin. "No one ever has before."

Victor tried to speak, but Michael cut him off with a quick kiss. Then he slid out of bed, pulled on his sweats, and left to shower. He had a café to visit today, a local hangout known for their pastries and tea lattes, and he didn't have time to explain his brokenness to Victor. Because if he did, he would unveil his own hideous secret—that he craved what he'd always prevented himself from having—and even though he was sure Victor had seen it, spelled out in blood licked from Michael's skin, it wasn't something he was sure Victor would understand if he tried to explain it himself. If he had to say it out loud.

Being fucked like he was loved wasn't the problem but wanting to be loved was.

Because love was a dangerous, sharp-toothed thing, and if Michael didn't rip it up from the roots, if he didn't bury it while he still had the chance, it might tear him apart again.

He showered quickly. Dried off and brushed his teeth, styled his hair and tried to ignore how Victor's eyes trailed him as he pulled a thermal top over his head, followed by his black coat.

Victor gathered a breath.

"I'll be back in a bit," Michael blurted. He tried to smile and leaned across the bed to kiss him. Victor's lips were careful, hesitant. "Want anything while I'm out?"

He nodded, expression strung between confusion and caution, claws gentle on Michael's jaw. "A lemon," he whispered. "If you wouldn't mind."

"Just one?"

"Just one."

"Yeah, sure." Another chaste kiss. Another pointed look.

*I see you*, Victor said with his eyes. *I know you're running.*

Michael left two minutes before his Lyft arrived. He watched Port Lewis pass by the window and made small talk with the handsome driver. He had a wave tattooed on his arm and scars on his neck, and Michael wondered if he was a witch—one of the secrets Port Lewis hid beneath bone and brine and constant storms. There was an amethyst cluster in the cupholder. A small, curved ring in the shape of a claw sat beside it.

"Cool ring," Michael said.

The driver plucked it from the cupholder and slid it over his middle finger, careful of the sharpened silver tip. "It's my boyfriend's," he said, masking a nervous swallow with a shrug. They stopped along the curb downtown. "Welcome to Port Lewis, by the way."

"Thanks, man. Any Crescent Café recommendations?"

"The rooibos milk tea is good. A little too sweet for me, but Ryder loves it," he said. He had a good smile and kind eyes and wore a silver seashell pendant around his neck.

Michael didn't know who Ryder was, but he smiled and nodded anyway. Boyfriend, probably. The way the driver said his name certainly made it sound that way. "Thanks again." He shut the passenger door and stepped onto the sidewalk as the Subaru cruised away.

The streets were damp. Cobblestone pathways snaked between eclectic buildings. A pizza parlor with a brick wall sat on the corner and neon bulbs lit the movie theater's sign two blocks away. Downtown was technically on the south side of Port Lewis, a three-block stretch of shops and eateries catering to locals and tourists alike. Garden boxes lazed in a fenced area between two shopfronts. Dark green vines curled from the soil and bird houses hung from thin chains on low-hanging tree branches. Soggy maple leaves in varying shades of orange, maroon, and deep mahogany were plastered to the cement.

Crescent Café had a crooked sign painted in swirling cursive. The silhouette of a cat lazed in the C of Café and a bell at the top of the door chimed when he pushed it open. Small lamps hung over glass cases filled with decadent pastries—cupcakes topped with buttercream frosting, pies with extravagant latticework, scones and sun-shaped cookies and star-shaped macarons. Tables with mismatched chairs were littered in the adjacent room. Colorful paintings adorned the wall next to quirky framed photographs.

"Welcome," the woman behind the counter said. Her yellow apron was decorated with enamel pins and the pale gray sweater underneath was a stark contrast to her rich, dark skin. She adjusted the white scarf tied around her shaved head, smile relaxed and warm. "You're a face I haven't seen before."

"Yeah, hi." Michael glanced at the chalkboard menu above her head and fiddled with his phone. "I'm Michael, I just moved here a couple weeks ago. I was actually interested in writing a piece about this place. Is the owner around?"

"You're looking at her," she said. Her smile parted into a grin. Michael stepped forward to shake her hand, but he realized a moment too late that letting her touch him was a mistake. "I'm Thalia Darbonne." Her voice dropped away at the end. Fingers squeezed his tight. Energy slipped over his skin, as cold and brittle as fresh snow. "So, you're *that* Michael. I've heard about you," she whispered, eyes narrowed. "Michael Gates."

He swallowed nervously. "I've heard about you too."

"And how much have you heard about me?"

"Enough to know you're in charge; not enough to know you owned this café."

"Christy told me you were pretty brave last weekend."

"Technically, I was pretty drunk," Michael said.

At that, Thalia's grin turned into a quiet laugh. She released his hand and tilted her head back to look at the menu. "You mentioned a piece? Are you a journalist?"

Michael watched her lashes flick, how the bow of her top lip was full and pinched on her wide mouth. She was beautiful and powerful, and if he remembered correctly, a big deal in this small town. "Blogger, actually. Do you mind if I take pictures?"

"Not at all. Can I get you something to drink? A cookie, maybe?"

"I'll take a rooibos milk tea. And yeah, sure, a cookie would be great."

"Do you mind if I join you?" Thalia's raised brow was a challenge, and her question wasn't much of a question at all. Air whipped restlessly inside the cozy café. "Honey for your tea?"

"That'd be great."

"Feel free to take pictures of whatever you'd like." She handed his change back to him, which he dumped straight into the tip jar. "I'll bring your order out to you."

There wasn't much expectation when it came to Thalia. He didn't know what she wanted and whatever it was, he doubted he could give it to her. He'd been there that night. He saw what he saw. Felt what he felt. Did what he did. Victor's magic still curled tightly inside him where blood stained his fragile, human bones. There was no taking that back. No doing away with it. And from the way Thalia had looked at him, intrigued and attentive, she was plenty aware of that already.

He took pictures of the chalkboard menu, angled his phone to catch the glint off the edible glitter dusted over the cupcakes in the case, and snapped a photo of the light beaming in through the window onto a lonely square table where he eventually sat.

A femme wearing chunky headphones typed on a rose gold laptop in the corner. An older couple chatted quietly and shared a thick piece of strawberry cake at a table along the far wall. Michael watched a few people walk by the window, wrapped in scarves and beanies and coats. Halloween decorations were placed in windows and hung from streetlamps, the holiday still far enough away to feel distant, but soon enough to make the sun-shaped pumpkin cookie Thalia set in front of him look appropriately festive. And it smelled delicious.

"So." She sat down, hands folded casually around a steaming mug. "You're dating Victor Lewellyn."

*Just like that, huh?* Michael sipped his tea and lifted one shoulder in a shrug. "Yeah, I guess I am."

"You understand what he is?"

"For the most part."

Thalia's lips twitched into a smirk. "Did he tell you how new I am to this whole thing?"

"He didn't know you became queen or whatever because he was excommunicated by his own friends and family," Michael said, bitterness laced tightly through each syllable. "But he did mention you. Said he was friends with your brother."

"Lewellyns do things differently than Darbonnes. If it were up to me, he'd already have a permanent glamour talisman and a tether point outside the house. But it's not, and he is what he is, and there's nothing I can do to change that." She pushed the plate toward him. "Nothing you can do to change it either."

"I'm aware of that." He broke a piece off the cookie and popped it into his mouth. Spicy cinnamon and sweet vanilla mingled with pumpkin and nutmeg. "What's a tether point?"

"A way for him to travel outside the place where he integrated with his demon. It wouldn't be far without a proper attachment, but he'd be able to stay in Port Lewis, have his own space, go to dinner or movies if he wanted to. Unfortunately, Margo won't allow that."

"Margo's the queen Lewellyn bee, right?"

Thalia nodded. "If she knew he'd formed an intimate relationship with someone outside the clans, she'd have words for him, I'm sure."

"She doesn't have any control over him anymore," Michael said matter-of-factly. Thalia's dark eyes snapped to his, narrowed and stern. He looked back at her, hoping his feigned confidence came across as strongly as he needed it to. "And she definitely doesn't have any control over me."

Her lips pressed into a thin line. A thick, penciled-in brow climbed toward her headscarf. "You're right," she said softly, impressed. "That's probably what scares her. She can't control him. But you could."

Michael paused, the curve of his mug set against his mouth.

"You know that, don't you? It would be a simple spell. Some blood, a few words, a—"

"I don't want anything to do with that," he snapped. His teeth clicked and his cheeks flushed, and his knuckles whitened around the warm mug. "Literally, nothing. I..." He finished his tea, gaze flicking from Thalia toward the window. Frustration came skidding out of him, snarled and honest. "Why is it hard to believe me and him might actually *like* each other? You think I wanna put a collar on him, Vassa thinks he wants to bleed me and screw me and leave me, my sister thinks I'll never be anything but..." He gathered an annoyed breath and stopped in his tracks, letting the words fester and thicken between them. "I want to know about his world, yeah, who wouldn't? But I care about him, believe it or not. I have feelings for him that don't stem from"—he gestured to her with a flick of his wrist—"your hocus pocus bullshit."

Thalia tilted her head, regarding him skeptically. He ate the rest of the cookie, gaze still pointed out of the window. People walked from shop to shop. Sunlight filtered through cloud cover and another dark storm billowed in the distance. He went over what he'd said, each harsh word, every quick breath. Brave and stupid, he thought. Reckless and fucking ridiculous.

He closed his eyes and opened his mouth to apologize, but she cut him off.

"I believe you," Thalia said. Surprise filtered through, as if she hadn't expected to feel however she was feeling. Michael could relate. "Haven't you only known him for a few weeks?"

"Two and a half. Trust me, I know how it sounds. I'm not..." He licked his lips and sighed. "I'm not used to this. *At all*. At fucking all, okay? I didn't expect—I mean, none of this was supposed to happen."

"I know what it's like to love someone you know you shouldn't," she said.

"It's not just about loving him, it's—"

Michael stopped. Everything stopped. He didn't breathe or blink or move. His heart might have stopped too, stuttering and kicking in his chest, tripped up by his own voice, his own unsettled secret and stubborn reluctance.

Love did not exist in bullet-shaped timeframes. *This is too soon*, he thought. *This is too sudden.*

"It's about Essence and the house and how we're supposed to make this work when everyone around us is sure it won't," Michael said. He leveled his voice, forging a sense of calm and keeping it close—a mask he could hide behind. Love was too frightening to consider. Not yet. Not like this.

"Victor doesn't belong to a clan anymore, not really." Thalia didn't press him. Her eyes were kind and knowing, a look he'd seen on people far wiser than him. "He's on his own. It's a blessing and a curse."

"How so?"

"Because he doesn't need to ask for permission. He can do as he pleases, which *could* have potential consequences, of course." She tilted her head and shrugged. "But he's the son of a second. There isn't much anyone could do."

Michael remembered the night on the balcony, the first time he'd kissed Victor. "Yeah, he told me that. He's also a demon, so."

Thalia laughed, winded and sore. "That too."

"Why are you telling me this?" He shifted in his seat, turning from the window toward Thalia. "I'm just the guy who lives in that old house. I'm not involved in any of..."

He didn't know the term. Business? Fuckery? Clan drama? "I mean, I'm not special. I don't have power or magic or..." Thalia lifted her hand and shushed him, glancing to the occupied tables in the quiet café. He lowered his voice. "Any teeth in whatever fight this is."

Her eyes ran across him. Once, twice, a third time, darting around his face, over his neck and chest. "Those marks on your throat—those are from blood magic, aren't they?"

He immediately covered them, self-conscious and caught. Thin scabs bit his palm.

"That's what I thought," she whispered. Her smile softened and she heaved an impatient sigh. "There isn't a fight, Michael. There's stigma and rules and things we can't change overnight. You're involved with someone whose existence breaks the natural order of things, and unfortunately, Margo Lewellyn has used her authority to make room for the only other anomaly, besides Victor, I know of."

"And who might that be?" Michael asked through clenched teeth.

"A Fire witch who can raise the dead," she bit back. "Who's alive because of an attachment with a demonic entity. My partner's little brother."

"That's convenient."

"It is," she said, and leaned forward, expression stern and cold. "Because that means *I* have the authority to make room for Victor."

Michael's jaw slackened. None of this made sense. *None of it*. But he knew a deal when he heard one. He knew the mischievous glint in Thalia's eyes. He knew the pale scars peeking from under her collar and curving over the top of her hands. She lifted her brows, and Michael realized he knew the look she wore because it meant *this is a secret, this is wrong, this will come with punishment*, and he was fluent in that language.

"This is your chance to go home, pack your things, and get out while you still can." Thalia did not blink. She held his gaze confidently. Her invisible magic locked cruelly around his throat and tightened. "It will be the only chance you have. Do you understand?"

"And if I don't leave?" He stared back at her, fingers buckled into tight fists in his lap.

"Then you'll be tied to that decision for a long, long time."

The bell above the door chimed.

Thalia gave him one last, lingering glance, a warning and an invitation, before she stood and said, "I look forward to your piece about the café."

Michael nodded. The Darbonne matriarch walked away, shoulders back, arms loose at her side. She looked regal, as if her feet hovered on each step, barely touching the floor. If he looked close enough, he swore he saw her aura, a flicker of white light curving around her body like a halo.

He'd been in Port Lewis less than a month and already the town had its hooks in him. Already he was involved in things he never knew existed. Already he'd fallen for someone powerful and vicious, someone who had once been a witch and was now something worse.

*You're a fool*, he thought. *A damn fool.*


RAIN SPLATTERED THE sidewalk.

Michael hadn't expected the afternoon to bring lightning storms and a downpour, but it did. He took shelter in a bookstore first, ducked into a novelty shop after, and finally found the brewery where he'd had dinner at with Janice. His coat wasn't entirely soaked through, but it was wet enough to make him shiver.

MICHAEL: *I'm here.*
JANICE: *I'll be there in 5.*

He'd agreed to meet her after three long-winded, apologetic texts that straddled the line between passive-aggressive and empathetic. Fingertips rubbed the small, round lemon he kept in his inside pocket. Thoughts circled back to Thalia's regal stance and tempered strength, how she'd been open enough with him to get him to talk and reserved enough to keep him curious. Michael felt played, like he was treading water in a pool filled with sharks.

MICHAEL: *I ran into Thalia today.*
VICTOR: *Oh?*
MICHAEL: *I got your lemon too*
VICTOR: *Did Thalia say anything to you?*
MICHAEL: *she said A LOT to me*

"Hey, sorry. There was no parking." Janice shrugged off her jacket and hung it on a hook by the door. Her eyes landed on him once, a fleeting glance that spoke to her nervousness. She bit her lip and stood on her tiptoes. "Any seats in the bar?"

"I think I saw a high top." He hung his coat and trailed after her.

Sometimes their relationship was strained. Not sometimes—often. But this was new. This was Michael's heart on the table and Janice knowing she could drive a fork through it if she wanted to. They ordered drinks and a pretzel and sat across from each other. Maybe they both expected an apology. Maybe neither of them deserved one. He didn't know, but if he didn't disarm the situation soon, he wasn't sure if he'd ever be able to.

"Sorry I've been avoiding you," he said.

"It's typical," she said. Her mouth was set and straight, eyebrows slouched and tense. "I'm sorry about Christian."

"Which part are you sorry for? The part where I was sleeping with a married man or the part where you made me feel like shit over it?"

"Both, I think. You put yourself in a bad situation and I was too pissed to notice when it became abusive. I thought you were just doing what you normally did—getting laid, showing off, being stupid."

"*Abusive* is a strong word." Michael drained half his beer. *Abusive is the only word*.

"Did he ever hit you?"

"Not..." *Without my permission*. Lie. *Hard*. Lie. *When we weren't in bed*. The worst truth.

"Did he ever *hurt* you?"

He leaned away from the table as a server set their pretzel between them. Memories came and went, too fast to grab. The time he met Christian at a hotel and Michael had to call Janice to pick him up because he couldn't drive. Christian's rough mouth. How he'd wrenched Michael's hands behind his back and slammed him down. He'd told his sister the tremors were from too much coke. Truthfully, Christian had shattered a lamp, they'd screamed at each other, and the sex had been too painful to qualify as *makeup* anything. It'd been hateful. Mean. Spiteful. And it'd left him afraid.

Michael hadn't said anything about the handprints on his thighs or the soreness in his hips or the lump in his throat to Janice that night. He hadn't said anything at all.

"I kept going back," he blurted. His eyes slipped shut and he shook his head. "When he did, I always went back, so it doesn't matter if he hurt me or not."

"I don't get you, Michael... I wish I did, but, I just—why didn't you say something to me? Why didn't you tell—"

"It's over, all right? Done. Buried. Can we move on?" He glanced at her, blinking away brutal memories. "Please?"

Janice reached across the table and grabbed his wrist, the same wrist she *always* grabbed, where his scar could press against her fingertips, a cruel, blatant reminder of how he traded strength for weakness when it mattered most. She hiccupped on a breath, steadied her voice. "I'm your sister," she said softly. "And I am telling you this now. Right now. However he made you feel and whatever he said to keep you coming back, you are worth more than that. Do you understand?"

Michael refused to look at her. Not because she was right, but because a part of him—buried, deep, *deep*—still believed she was wrong. "I hear you."

"Do you *understand* me?"

"Yeah, I do. I get it. Can we eat our pretzel and never, *ever* talk about this again?"

Slowly, she let go of his wrist. "Is... I mean, I hate to ask this, but is Victor anything like—"

"Victor is kind. He's gentle and patient," Michael assured. He drained the rest of his beer. Tore off a piece of the pretzel. Smothered it in mustard. "And he gives me exactly what I need."

Janice raked her fingers through her hair. "Good." She cleared her throat, sipped her beer, stared at the table and tapped her fingernails on a damp coaster. "I'm assuming you two are *actually* dating now?"

"Were we doing something else before?"

"You tell me. You're the one who'd rather eat a wasp's nest than change your relationship status on Facebook."

Michael laughed. Anxiety still pooled in him, cold and unwanted, but at least Janice smiled back at him, and at least he could order another beer, and at least the marks under his clothes had been left by someone who made him feel wanted. Who made him feel craved and encouraged. Who made him *feel*.

"How's your zebra?" Michael asked, baring his teeth in a grin.

Janice rolled her eyes. "Still buying me coffee and still making weird-ass sounds." She smoothed a napkin over her lap, smile strained but there, as if she'd shaken off the apprehension and replaced it with playfulness. He hoped they stayed like this, *just* like this, laughing and teasing each other and letting his past with Christian stay buried with the rest of his mistakes.

The pretzel was gone too quickly, so they ordered another appetizer and two more beers. Michael told her about Victor—the pastry chef part, not the demon part. He told her about Victor's tenderness. How vulnerability tasted different with him than it ever had with anyone else.

"Maybe that's because you've never let yourself be vulnerable before," Janice said.

Michael nodded. "Yeah, maybe."

*Yeah, definitely.*

They talked about sex and life and college and futures. Michael tried not to think about the things Thalia had said to him. *Get out while you still can.* He tried not to imagine what was coming, because something was coming. Something that would stay with him.

"Port Lewis is kinda cool, huh? Spooky," Janice teased, wiggling in her seat. "Like Salem or Amityville. It's got history."

"History." Michael finished his beer and nodded. "That's one way to put it."



WIND SNAPPED AT Michael's cheeks. He shielded his cigarette and took a long drag, watching lights flicker through the trees from his balcony. Night darkened the neighborhood. Stars settled in the sky despite the early hour, a promise that autumn would bleed into a long, merciless winter.

Choices stuck to Michael's ribs. They came with unanswerable questions and unknowable consequences, a world he'd never imagined and a life he wasn't sure would welcome him.

But he'd made up his mind and there was no changing it now.

Smoke drifted from his parted lips. He didn't notice the way the air shifted for Victor anymore. How the night deepened in his presence. How time warped and bent, causing silence and stillness to miss their cues. But he did notice the way Victor paused before he kissed the almost-healed cut on Michael's neck, how he hesitated, hands featherlight on Michael's waist, and stayed quiet.

Their bodies were inches apart. Heat from Victor's chest seeped through Michael's thermal shirt and warmed his back. Another long drag. Another held breath. Another exhale.

"Thalia told me to leave tonight," Michael said softly. Claws traced his hipbones, playing absently with the belt loops on his jeans. "Said this was my last chance to get out."

"Why didn't you?" Victor rested his horns on Michael's shoulder and let out a sad, breathy sigh.

"Because I said I'd bring you a lemon."

Victor huffed a laugh. "That's why, huh?"

He smothered the cigarette butt under his shoe. "Because I want you to blindfold me." The words were hushed and weak. *Don't tremble.* He swallowed hard and closed his eyes. "And I want you to tie my wrists, and I want you to do whatever you want to me."

"What if I wanted to ask you questions?"

"I'd answer them."

Victor shook his head. Worry or something close tripped into his voice. "And if I wanted to whip you with a belt?"

Michael's nostrils flared. His breath came short, throat tight and lungs aching. "I'd let you."

"What if I wanted to bite you until you bled? Choke you until you blacked out? What about then?"

A weak sound built in his throat. "Victor, c'mon, please—"

"Tell me what this is about."

"It's complicated, I just—"

"You ran out of here with your tail between your legs this morning. I want the truth, Michael," he said, pressing the words close to Michael's ear, gentle and pleading.

"Because the last time I gave up control, it wasn't by choice," he snapped. "Control was ripped from me in a fucking hotel room by the only other person I've ever loved, and I went back to him after." Michael didn't turn around. He chewed on the inside of his cheek and tried to even his breathing, to stay calm, to allow himself the chance to be honest with someone. With Victor. "Christian…" He had never said it out loud because he'd never believed it was true. And still, here, now, he stomped his foot because he couldn't find the courage to say it.

"You asked me not to say his name," Victor said.

Michael turned around, jaw clenched and hand digging in his pocket for another cigarette. "I went back to Christian after he date-raped me," he said, the words skidding out of him, violent and sour. "I went back to him after he told me I was worthless, after he held me down on a filthy bed in the middle of nowhere. I still remember the taste of his fucking wedding ring because he…" He lit the cigarette and took an angry, quick drag. His voice lowered, blown open by an exhale, words mingling with smoke. "He put his hand over my mouth to keep me quiet."

Victor stayed completely still. His horns blended in with the night, black and jagged, shadowed beautifully over his dark hair. His pupils shook, eyes flicking back and forth, as if he'd remembered something important. Something that wasn't his.

"Don't look at me like that, please, *please* don't fucking look at me like that," Michael said. He took another drag. Tears brimmed over his lashes and heat crackled in his chest, embers burning hot in his fast-beating heart. "I didn't fuck you to make myself feel better, okay? I'm not a charity case."

"Of course you're not," Victor said, wounded and breathless. "You never have been. Not then, not now."

"I'm not broken because of it. He didn't take that from me—my body, sex, happiness. He doesn't get to ruin that. He doesn't get to screw up what I have with you, okay?" Michael hated crying. *He hated it.* If he could carve his tear ducts out and toss them over the balcony, he would. But he turned toward the wall instead, mouth wobbling, eyes stinging, and swatted tears away as they fell.

"Have you told anyone else?" Victor eased closer, carefully, slowly.

He shook his head, cigarette between his lips, fingers trembling around the filter. "I almost told my sister tonight, but it's old shit that happened two years ago. She would've just felt bad and it wasn't her fault, so."

"And you want me to control you, right? That's where we're at?"

"This morning you asked me if I'd ever tell you why I"—he gestured to his red-rimmed, glassy eyes with an absent wave of his hand—"do this sometimes. The first time we did blood magic together, I told you I didn't feel powerful enough to be in your world. I asked you to own me, I told you to hurt me, and I don't want you to think I equate *you* with *him* because I asked for that." Another drag. Another long, weighty exhale. "But I don't know how to let myself be vulnerable with someone who actually gives a shit about me, okay? I left Christian. I traveled. I slept with other people and tried to get over it and told myself I wouldn't go back, because who the hell would go back to the person who did that to them? Me. I would."

"That doesn't mean you deserved it," Victor said.

"Doesn't it, though?" Michael spun around, flicking the cigarette again and again. He chewed anxiously on his lip, staring at Victor's gold eyes and strong jaw.

Victor disappeared and reappeared in front of him. Black smoke drifted from the bow of his lips and his sloped nose. His breath hit Michael's mouth, hands sure and grounding on his hips. "No, it doesn't."

"I'm sorry." Michael's voice lowered into a whisper. He rested his forehead on Victor's shoulder and handed over the cigarette when Victor slid his fingers around it.

A strong arm curled around his back. "What're you sorry for?"

"Throwing my bullshit at your feet when I've known you for less than a month."

"Look at me."

Michael didn't want to. He closed his eyes and kept his face buried in Victor's neck, hiding, like always. Victor flicked the cigarette into a puddle next to the potted lily and took Michael's chin between his ashy fingers, tugging until his face was exposed.

"Look at me," he said again. This time, Michael did as he was told. "I've spent almost every day with you for the past few weeks. I've slept beside you." His claw trailed the corner of Michael's mouth. "Showered with you. Talked with you for hours. Seen your memories." Heat rushed into Michael's cheeks, but he didn't stir, just stayed there, pliant and obedient, safe and held. "Shouldn't that be enough?"

"Yeah, it should be," he said under his breath.

"I've held you down, covered your mouth, restrained you—I've made you bleed." Victor slid his palm to his cheek, holding his face carefully. "Michael, if I've ever hurt you, please—"

"I asked you to," Michael interjected. He leaned into Victor's hand, turned and caught the curve of his thumb with his lips. "I *wanted* you to."

Silence filled the minuscule space between them. Wind died. The night did not move or breathe. Rain refused to fall, as if the storm had stopped in its tracks and refused to interrupt them.

"Tell me exactly what you want." He tipped Michael's head back, angling him where he wanted.

"Tie my wrists," Michael whispered. Victor dragged his lips over Michael's cheek and kissed his jaw. "Blindfold me." A kiss to his neck. The scrape of teeth on his ear. "I'm giving you permission to do whatever you want."

"Tell me you want to be out of control."

"I want to be out of control."

"What's your safe word?" Victor opened his mouth over the flexed tendon in Michael's throat.

"Tulip."

"What's my name?"

"Victor."

A low, wicked growl came from deep in Victor's chest.

Michael slid his hands over Victor's shoulders, curled them around the back of his head, into his hair, and clutched the base of his horns. "Allocer," he said softly.

Magic swept around them. Michael's heart kicked hard behind his ribs. Moonlight cut through the clouds, illuminating the balcony and his bedroom and them, eager and raw, torn open by a secret Michael hadn't known what to do with. An ugly, confusing thing that lived on the dark side of his heart, misshapen and heavy—a black hole with sharp teeth that had been chewing on him for days and weeks and months and years.

Michael had been running when he left Arizona. He'd been looking for a way out, a new start, a clean slate, and somehow, he'd found all those things in a haunted attic, tucked on a bookshelf, written in messy ink.

*Victor Lewellyn.*

The lights in his bedroom went out the moment they stumbled inside. Victor snapped his fingers and a candle on the dresser sparked. His wide hands gripped Michael's hips, claws stinging freckled skin, digging in hard before he pushed him backward.

*Deep breaths.* Michael didn't think about what he'd said to Janice at the brewery. *You're safe.* His back hit the bed. He didn't think of his wounds or his past or his hurt. *You're allowed to have this.* Victor's breath was hot in his mouth, knees on either side of him, tugging at his shirt, his jeans. *Let go.*

When Victor pinned his arms above his head, Michael pushed against him, desperate to feel the strain, the thrum of energy pulsing in the air, the jab of adrenaline spiking through his stomach. When Victor held him down and kissed him hard, Michael's bones vibrated. His skin flushed. He licked into Victor's mouth, craning away from the bed to chase another kiss, another sharp bite to his bottom lip, another too-hot breath and raspy growl. Claws pinched his wrists. Hipbones dug into his pelvis.

Michael looked at him, undone, shaking and breathless, and did not move when Victor's pupils stretched into long diamonds. He watched the darkness turn and twist, becoming corporeal, and he didn't flinch when the shadows wrapped around his wrists. They were covered in thorns, reminiscent of vines, dotted with budding flowers and smoky leaves.

Victor waited for him to nod, then tied a thin scarf around Michael's eyes, shrouding him in blackness. He pushed against the shadowed restraints and they warmed, tightening until the thorns bit his skin. Relief followed the pain, a senseless, utterly selfish indulgence. The bedroom quieted. Flames popped on the candlewick. Weight disrupted the floorboards, pulling creaks and groans from the old wood.

Like this—bare on a bed, restrained by magic, blind and vulnerable and at Victor's mercy—Michael could do nothing but tremble and wait. His knees pressed together. Anxiety sparked in the depths of him, awakened by the cold air on his skin, by the silence and the sound of his own breath.

"Vic?" His name slipped past Michael's lips in the shape of a whimper.

The bed dipped again. Michael held his breath, waiting. Victor didn't move. He shifted until his thighs touched the outside of Michael's hips, but he stayed still—watching, maybe. Looking down at him. The thought made Michael squirm, made him think of every scar and tattoo, every imperfection and odd-shaped freckle. But before he could speak again, Victor kissed him. He opened his mouth wide for deeper, wetter kisses, traced the edge of Victor's teeth with his tongue, and tipped his head back when Victor broke away, placing his mouth elsewhere. On Michael's throat. In a line down his sternum. Teeth sharp around his nipple, biting hard. Again on his ribcage, working a bruise there.

Michael could barely breathe. He tried to wrench his arms away, desperate to push his fingers through Victor's hair, but the dark, alchemical vines tightened, keeping him still. Every touch was unexpected. Lips on his stomach. Claws digging into his sides. Victor's mouth on his cock, brief and barely there. A ruthless bite to his inner-thigh that caused his back to bend and his breath to catch.

Every sensation was *more* like this. Visceral. Electric.

At one point, Victor lifted his hips. He kissed the skin beneath his hipbone, the back of his thigh, the base of his cock, lower, *lower*—pressed his tongue inside him, licked and kissed until Michael was a shaking, whimpering mess. Everything was too much. Too sudden. Too good. When Victor eased him back to the bed, Michael expected another harsh bite, for a palm to crack across his thigh, something sharp to slice his skin. But instead, Victor hovered over him, his breath warm and stunted on Michael's jaw. Something slender touched his thigh, rubbed behind his balls. A blunt, smooth object circled his hole and slid inside him. Unfamiliar. Ribbed and slick and warm.

"Rose quartz wand," Victor clarified. "Don't hold your breath."

Michael exhaled. Inhaled. Exhaled. Victor worked the wand slowly and whispered something close to his ear. Latin, maybe. His voice was layered with different sounds, wind through trees, stones on concrete, hisses and growls and sighs. The moment he said it, heat followed his fingertips, wrapped around the wand, and rushed into Michael. His back arched, jaw slack, mouth open, and he yelped on a startled, gasped breath. His hips jumped, searching for more of Victor—more of his crystal wand.

Victor hushed him. "Easy," he said, gently, effortlessly.

"What the hell was that?" Michael heaved in breath after breath, grateful for Victor's lips on his cheek, his jaw, close to his mouth.

"Heat spell. Move your hips—yeah, like that." He kissed Michael again, a deep, long kiss, and Michael did as he was told, rocking down onto the wand in time with Victor's short, shallow thrusts. The heat came in waves, moving through him whenever Victor pushed the wand against his prostate and fading when he eased it away.

He didn't know what he looked like right then, fucking himself on the toy in Victor's hand, writhing and moaning, held to the bed by dark magic. But he loved the way it felt—suspended and safe, and completely, endlessly controlled.

"Are you close?" Victor asked.

Michael nodded. He tipped his head back, searching for Victor's lips. He couldn't see—couldn't reach for him, but Victor only left him wanting for a moment, then he was there, prying at Michael's mouth, kissing the breathless whimper from him.

The wand disappeared. Michael whined and ground down against the bed. "N-no, don't stop, c'mon—"

"Whatever I want, remember?"

The bed shifted. Victor stroked his tense stomach, felt over his thighs, followed his hips to his ribs, his chest to the inside of his arms. Desire settled deep in his bones, an ache that unfurled toward his skin. Everywhere Victor touched, Michael leaned toward him. When Victor's fingers found the soft indention of his elbows, he pushed into them. When claws tickled the hollow of his throat, he flexed and stretched and bared himself, panting and wound tight.

Victor's touches softened. He left kisses on Michael's shoulders. Dragged his hand down the flat expanse of his torso and pressed his thumb into the soft divot below his hipbone. Pleasure curled tightly inside him, throbbing low in his stomach, between his legs, at the base of his spine.

Michael yielded completely. He relaxed when Victor guided his legs apart, breathed as he listened to a cap click, nodded when Victor paused to stroke his hip, and bit back a moan when he finally, *finally* pushed inside him. He strained against the black vines. Thorns stung his skin.

Victor pulled Michael's hips, tugging him further into his lap, and guided each movement. He rolled into Michael—painfully deep, blissfully slow. Michael moved with him, canting his hips to meet every rhythmic thrust, listening to Victor's breath quicken and his moans turn raspy, and wanted desperately to touch him.

"Vic, please," Michael choked out.

Victor made it last and last. His movements were honeyed and patient, keeping Michael teetering on the edge, straddling the line between satisfaction and restless, drawn-out pleasure. Before Michael could beg or squirm, his thighs were tipped toward his chest, looped over Victor's arms, and the blindfold was pushed away.

It didn't register that the vines around his wrists were gone until Michael reached for Victor's face, until they were breathing the same air, eyes locked, with Michael's trembling hands gripping his cheeks. Never had pleasure felt as pure and unrestrained as it did right then, and never had sex or intimacy tethered itself to how Michael felt about someone like it did right then, as he gasped and quivered, enduring the hot, familiar pulse of Victor coming inside him. Victor grabbed his wrists and pressed them against the bed again, slotting his long, bony fingers between Michael's knuckles. He made the softest sounds, breathless gasps and wounded growls echoing from deep in his chest. And when it was over, he kissed his way down ink and scars, relaxed and loose and eager, and wrapped his lips around Michael's cock. Two fingers slid inside him, rough and fast, and it was enough to send him tumbling over the edge, clutching Victor's horns and crying out, bowed off the bed with his heels digging into the mattress.

Blood trickled from tiny tears in his skin where the black, smoky vines had squeezed too tight. He closed his eyes, tracking each kiss Victor pressed to his body. One on his thigh. Another on his hip. Dusted along the atlas moth, over his clavicle. He sighed, warm and sated, shifting on the bed as it dipped beside him.

Victor's palm settled on his cheek. He thumbed away wetness gathered at the corner of Michael's eye. "Hey," he rasped and tugged until Michael looked at him. The claw curving from his thumb tapped Michael's temple. "What's going on up here?"

"Nothing important."

"I doubt that."

Michael's body hummed, settling into the hazy effects of a proper afterglow. "I told you to do whatever you wanted and you..." He realized what he was about to say and sighed, because of course that's what he'd be thinking. Of course that's what Michael Gates would wonder about. "You weren't very rough."

"Were you expecting me to be?"

*I was expecting punishment.* "I don't know, maybe."

"Are you disappointed?" Victor's brow furrowed.

He turned on his side and inched closer, hand pressed against Victor's broad, warm chest, nose to nose. "That's a joke, right?" His lips quirked into a smile. "You're the best fuck of my life, Victor Lewellyn. Congratulations. I'll get you a medal."

A coy grin curved across Victor's face. "Not everything has to hurt." He nuzzled his face into the pillow, arms thrown over Michael's smaller frame, and kissed his forehead. "Not that I'm not a fan of your teeth and nails, and not that I don't like throwing you into walls and holding you down, but I thoroughly enjoy making love to you."

Michael's nose scrunched. He snorted and rolled his eyes, trying and failing to keep the blush radiating in his cheeks from spreading to his ears. "Fuck you, c'mon, seriously?"

"You're one of those guys, aren't you?" Victor's grin widened, parting for a playful, teasing laugh. He slithered forward, pressing their bodies together, lips light on the corner of Michael's mouth. "Does it freak you out to hear someone say it? *Making love?*"

"It just feels fake," he mumbled, but that wasn't quite the truth. "Like something I'd hear at Bible camp."

"Is that right?" Victor leaned back to catch his gaze. His palm smoothed from Michael's cheek to his jaw, eyes bright and fiery in the dark.

He glanced around Victor's face. "Yeah, that's right. It feels fake because it's always sounded fake whenever anyone else said it, and it freaks me out because you make everything feel real. Even that."

The night was incredibly still. Moonlight lit the floorboards and dripped across the bed. Michael closed his eyes at the press of Victor's lips. They kissed slowly; tempered, fluid movements that deepened and lengthened. Michael's lashes fluttered. His chest ached, desperate for a breath he refused to take, burning and full. He opened his mouth for the stroke of Victor's tongue and curled closer, knee slipping between Victor's thighs, fingers tangled in his hair.

"You're easy to love," Victor said. He pulled Michael's bloody wrist to his mouth and kissed him there. It wasn't *I love you*—it didn't need to be. Maybe it was too soon for that, he thought. Or maybe, somehow, they'd passed the place where *I love you* would've changed them.

Perhaps it was too late for that.

Because Michael Gates had changed the moment he'd walked into the haunted house on Foxglove Lane.

# Part Eight: Hunters

THE STORM PASSED in the night.

Michael and Victor stayed awake, tangled close beneath the sheets, and whispered to each other about magic and traveling, music and gardening. Thunder clapped outside. Rain peppered the ceiling and the balcony. Victor told stories about the forest he used to frequent and the rituals he hosted there. At one point, he plucked a leaf from the long vine on a hanging caladium and closed his fingers around it, watching Michael carefully as he concentrated, then opened his hand again and revealed a small, violet butterfly fluttering in his palm. It landed on Michael's nose, settled between his two piercings, and then flew away to hide in the plant beside the dresser.

Lightning flashed. Michael straddled Victor's waist and took his picture. Then another. Another. Until Victor snatched the phone and pushed him down. Then it was Michael on display, comfortable and pink-cheeked, spread across the bed. They kissed and laughed, and Michael didn't shy from Victor's constant, gentle touches.

They fell asleep after the rain stopped. Morning brought mist over the balcony and a chill between the French doors and sent Michael burrowing under the blankets.

"Your feet are cold," Victor whined. He nuzzled the back of Michael's neck, arm tight around his chest.

"You'll live." They'd slept in later than usual. Michael remembered hearing a car door open and close hours ago and footsteps in the hallway soon after. But he'd dozed off again, content with staying in bed until Victor decided otherwise. "Coffee?"

"That would involve getting out of bed."

Michael turned onto his back and peeled his eyes open. "Yeah, sucks, huh?"

"Shower then coffee," Victor countered.

They stumbled into the bathroom with a sheet draped around them, clumsy and unhurried. The water was almost too hot. Steam billowed around them. Lips dragged across wet shoulders and kisses were littered on stomachs and thighs. Michael shivered, gasping as Victor hoisted him up, back pressed to the shower wall, legs wrapped around his waist, willing and relaxed and deliriously needy. His palm streaked through the fog on the glass door.

"I can't keep my hands off you," Michael whispered.

Victor smiled against his lips. "I'm not complaining."

They orbited each other constantly. In the shower, they were a tangled, too-sensual mess. Once the water stopped running, they toweled off, Michael brushed his teeth and Victor stood beside him, running product through his hair with sharp claws. They dressed in their separate rooms, but Victor found him downstairs as he always did, and ran his fingers across Michael's lower back, as he always did, and asked for extra sugar in his coffee, as he always did.

Passing touches grounded him to the here and now. Victor kissing his cheek. A tap to his shoulder. Victor nudging his hand on the table, silently asking for the jam.

*We're disgustingly domestic*, Michael thought.

But for once, he didn't feel the need to flee because of it.

"Where's that lemon—" Victor stopped. His gaze swept from Michael to the front door, and as if on cue, someone knocked.

Michael didn't move. He knew who it was—who it must be. But intention was what mattered, and he had no idea what she might want from them. Or take from them. He stood, heavy under Victor's watchfulness, made his way from the kitchen to the entryway, and opened the door.

Thalia wore an olive-green pantsuit. Thin, silver chains ringed her long throat, glistening like fine thread looped over sigils and runes. "Hello again, Michael."

"Hi." He didn't bother looking over his shoulder. The air fractured and the walls seeped wrongness. A shadow stretched across the floor beneath his feet. "What're you doing here?"

"I have a proposal," she said. She tilted her head, eyes rimmed in pale, glittery powder and cut by crisp, black liner. Her brow lifted, mouth quirked into a smile. "Can I come in?"

He stepped aside, allowing her to pass. But Victor didn't.

Michael closed the door and pressed his back against it, watching shadows blur and distort, weaving together on the floor and dripping quickly through the air. Victor appeared slowly, as if he'd been built from bronze liquid, standing poised and tall in front of Thalia.

"Thalia." Her name was a polite greeting in Victor's mouth. "What can I do for the Darbonne matriarch?"

She did not step back. Her shoulders stayed rigid and the energy around her whipped, plucking at the darkness curling from Victor's horns and hands. Michael was thankful for the solid door against his back. The magic throbbing around him was breath-stealing and absolute. It tilted the room. It felt watched. Deliberately volatile. Thalia tipped her chin over her shoulder and gave him a cool, patient once-over.

"You'll get used to it," she said.

"Yeah, well, I'm not used to it yet, so." One step at a time, Michael made his way into the kitchen. He poured more coffee into his mug and leaned against the counter to stay steady. "Thalia, you want some coffee?"

She took a seat at the kitchen table and shook her head, smile thin and forced. "No, thank you."

"Vic?"

Victor leaned against the sliding glass door, arms folded over his chest, and shook his head.

They waited. Michael watched Victor, Victor watched Thalia, and Thalia stared into the backyard, gaze distant and brows knitted. Michael sipped his coffee, and after seconds turned to minutes, and minutes seemed to slow, he opened his mouth and said, "What's this about?"

"You're a travel blogger, aren't you?" Thalia's eyes flicked toward him. She hadn't moved an inch, profile sharp and dignified.

Michael nodded. "Have been for a while, yeah."

"You can work from anywhere? Do your job on the road?"

He nodded again.

"And you"—she glanced at Victor—"are *extremely* powerful. Probably one of the strongest witches in Port Lewis."

"I'm more than a witch," Victor corrected.

Thalia steered her gaze toward the glass door again. "True..." The word came out hushed. She rubbed her fingers together, hesitating or deliberating—both, maybe. Finally, she licked her lips and straightened, breath quick, eyes narrowed, and Michael realized what she'd been doing all along—her bravado, her stance and expression. Thalia Darbonne had been gathering her courage, and Michael understood that feeling like no one else. "I have a lead on the Essence outbreak. From what we can see, the drugs are being created in Venice Beach. Esther, the dealer Christy and Vassa located, was last seen in downtown Los Angeles, slinging Essence at a fetish club."

Victor cocked his head, intrigued. "And?"

"And I'd like to hire someone to hunt them down," Thalia said, biting the words at him. Her confidence was a wildfire. Once it ignited, there was no beating back the flames. "Someone with no clan loyalty, no familial obligations, and no circle to worry about."

Michael's knuckles paled as he gripped the edge of the countertop.

Victor grinned, wild and wicked, and it reminded Michael that he was Allocer—horned and vicious and strong—as much as he was the man who had been in his bed last night. He clicked his tongue, a condescending noise meant for children. "Thalia Darbonne," he teased, purring her name. "You know it's forbidden to make deals with demons."

"We can help each other," she snapped. "You've already tethered with Michael. Use the bond to attach your energy to his physical body and you'll be able to go wherever he goes, it's a simple—"

"That is *not* simple," Victor growled.

"Tethered?" Michael hadn't meant to say anything. Not really. Not that quickly.

Thalia and Victor went quiet. They both looked at him. Thalia's dark eyes were riddled with apologies. Victor flexed his jaw, shooting Michael a sympathetic glance. Neither of them spoke. Not when Michael tapped his finger on the counter, not when he leaned forward, expectant and jittery, not when his lips parted and he exhaled a short, sharp breath.

"Can one of you fucking say something?"

"It means you share a future with Victor. You're magically bound." Thalia eased the words out slowly, one right after the other. "It's not uncommon, but I've never seen it happen with a demon before. You've... You've attached to his energy, probably by exposure to his blood, and now—"

Michael whipped toward Victor. "Did you know about this?" But before he finished the question, Victor jutted his chin at Thalia and asked, "Are you sure?"

Thalia nodded. "Christy felt it on you. Have you ever tethered before, Victor?"

"No," Victor said.

"And you haven't felt differently these past couple weeks?"

Victor's eyed Michael carefully. "I didn't know we tethered, if that's what you're asking."

"So, what?" Michael raked his fingers through his hair, trying to find movement, something, anything for him to focus on. "You want a bounty hunter? Is that it?"

"Hunters," Thalia corrected.

Excitement stirred where fear usually lived. Curiosity. Recklessness. Thick, eager *want*. Michael tried not to smile. He tried not to move, not to laugh or breathe too deeply. Magic, he thought. Magic and adventure and *Victor*.

Nothing had ever sounded more enticing.

"No," Victor said.

Michael hushed him.

"Michael, you would be bound to me for life—*life*, okay? Not an hour. Not a week or a year. You would be mine for—"

"Fine, great, we've got a deal," Michael said quickly, just to get it out of the way. He arched a brow and let a smile slip over his face as he met Thalia's eye. "We'd get paid for this, yeah?"

"Absolutely," Thalia said.

Victor stayed quiet, but his silence was louder than anything else in the room.

Michael nodded slowly. "And Victor would be welcome in the Darbonne clan?"

"Without question." Her back straightened, hands clasped in front of her. "I'm the matriarch, I make the rules. The elders will certainly raise their concerns, but in the end, my word is law."

"I'll need a glamour talisman," Victor said, his voice sudden and startling.

Thalia pulled a small, round stone from her right pocket and tossed it to him. Leather cord was strung through a drilled hole in its very center, and intricate, shallow carvings decorated both sides.

Victor narrowed his eyes. Clearly, he hadn't expected her to come prepared. But a twitch at the corner of his lips gave him away, a smile he could not mask. "We'll need transportation."

This time, Thalia reached into her left pocket and tossed him a key. "Range Rover. Stereo's shit, but there's an aux cable."

Victor hesitated, but only for a moment. He lifted his chin, watching her down the slope of his nose. "Boundaries?"

"Use your best judgement," she said.

"You're talking to a demon, Thalia."

"Then use Michael's best judgement."

Michael laughed, a single *ha*.

"I want this Essence ring turned to dust, Victor." Thalia slammed her palm on the table, leaving a slender, black credit card behind. She spoke as she took long strides toward the door. "Attach to Michael, pack necessities. You'll receive your first payment via wire transfer in the morning, and I'll expect to see you at the café before you leave."

"For what?" Victor called.

Thalia's laugh was light and genuine. Young. Strong. Relieved, maybe. "Breakfast, obviously."


THINGS MOVED QUICKLY after that.

Michael and Victor argued, snapping and barking at each other about choices and futures, consequences and danger. They paced around Michael's bedroom, slinging words like bullets, until Michael shoved Victor onto the bed and climbed on top of him.

They kissed desperately. Hungrily.

"You don't have to do this," Victor whispered between the parting of their lips, a cautious, mistaken thing.

"I want to do this," Michael said, and it was the truth.

Afternoon spun into night. Michael packed a duffle bag and a backpack. His hands trembled and his heart pounded, and he thought, *finally, this is it*.

A beginning.

Janice asked him to be careful. Telling her a hostel in Southern California had offered to sponsor a blog post and cover his travel expenses was much easier than the truth—he was about to open his heart and life and soul to a demon. She promised to care for his plants and tell their mom he was fine—*even if you're not*—and he'd promised to fill a bottle with sand from Venice Beach—*a little bit of sunshine*. They had dinner together, drank beers, laughed and tried to be what they needed to be for each other on that particular evening, in that particular house. They had to, didn't they? Trying was the start of something.

Night brought a candlelit bedroom.

Michael's chest fluttered and his pupils dilated. He tried to keep his breathing steady, but his lungs wouldn't cooperate. Every breath came short. He was hyperaware of every movement, every gust of wind against the window, every pop of a candlewick. Tiny, dancing flames lined the dresser and the nightstand, and tall, slender candles dripped wax onto the floor in the corners. Victor knelt at the edge of the bed, seated between Michael's legs. He held a black-handled blade in one hand. Shadows crossed his face, deep in the hollows beneath his cheekbones.

"Here?" Victor pressed the cold edge of the knife to Michael's thigh.

He swallowed and nodded. *Don't be afraid.* "There."

"Are you sure about this?" Victor leaned toward him, lips close enough to catch. His breath warmed Michael's chin. The blade slid over the curve of his thigh, higher, *higher*, until Michael gasped and closed his eyes. He gripped the mattress with both hands and nodded, closing the space between them to steal a kiss. Very quietly, Victor asked, "What's my name?"

"Victor," Michael whispered.

The first cut burned. Victor was careful, maneuvering the knife with ease and precision. After the third cut, the fourth, the fifth, Michael's breath turned choppy and his eyes watered. He whimpered, chewing hard on the inside of his cheek, helplessly strung between the desire to be touched and the urge to squirm away. Blood dripped into the crease of his knee and stained the white comforter, shone bright on Victor's fingertips and smeared over his skin.

Another slice. A quick, stinging nick. Comfortable, quaking heat built under the pain—pleasure undone.

Once the knife clattered on the floor, Michael looked down and found Allocer's sigil carved into his pale flesh. A breath was punched out of him at the sight. His head whirled and tilted. *It's done.* Lashes fluttered. *You're his.* There was no going back.

Victor pressed his lips to the center of the sigil, a searing, aching kiss. "Say it."

Michael took a deep breath. His eyes trailed Victor's chest, bronzed and beautiful in the dim candlelight. "Allocer, I..." Another gasp. Another tender, shaken moan as Victor opened his mouth over Michael's bloody thigh. "I-I... Fuck, I..." His heart raced. Dark magic clawed at his bones, chewed on veins and ligaments, dug needle-sharp into the space between each rib. *Say the words.* He tilted his head back and sucked in heavy, winded breaths. "I give myself to you," he whispered. Fingers wrapped around the warm, black bone of Victor's horn and tugged him into a rough kiss. "I give you my body," he said, wincing when a clawed hand gripped the fresh sigil on his thigh. "I give you my bones, my blood, and my allegiance."

Victor pulled back to look at him—his golden eyes, his red mouth—and pressed one single claw to his own chest. "I'm yours."

Michael opened his mouth and Victor dragged a bloody, clawed finger across his tongue.

Magic was not impossible. Neither was Victor. Neither was love.

They broke against each other, left bloody handprints on necks and chests and low on hips, kissed and bit and endured each other. Victor treated him like he was unbreakable, and Michael felt like he might've been. Unbreakable. Powerful. *Alive*. Victor left bruises on his ribcage, hickeys on his shoulders, a sigil on his thigh—he was careless with him, reckless and relentless, and Michael loved every moment of it. Every harsh bite. Every low growl against his throat, every hard swat to his ass, every kiss and touch and memory.

"You're mine," Michael said, perched in Victor's lap with his head thrown back, fingers tight in Victor's hair, bleeding and spent and *claimed*.

In the shower, the water turned pink at their feet.

In the morning, Victor tied the talisman—a garnet covered in spell work—around his neck. The charm disrupted the energy around him and stitched a tightly packed glamour over his horns and eyes and claws. Victor's bones softened. He looked tamer like this, human and acceptable. Michael ran his fingers through Victor's hair, cupped his cheek, brushed his thumb across the tips of his lashes.

"How do I look?" Victor asked and set his forehead against Michael's temple.

"Just as handsome as you did last night, don't worry," Michael said.

Victor smiled through another long, easy kiss.

They threw their bags into the car as the sun peeked over the horizon. Janice wished him a sleepy farewell, smacked a kiss to his cheek and told him to text her when they were halfway to Venice. Corey said goodbye as well, a friendly wave and shy, perfect smile.

At Crescent Café, Thalia handed them tea and coffee in large to-go cups, and paper bags stuffed with scones and muffins. "Be safe," she said. The closed sign still hung on the door and the café was dark except for the kitchen. "Keep me updated."

Morning turned the sky pink and mauve where it wasn't navy, and a transparent moon hung in the middle of the sky, clinging to the last threads of night. Michael watched Port Lewis pass by outside of the window, a blur of brick and stone, trees and moss, cliffs and mist. A black beanie hugged the back of his head and a beige scarf was coiled around his neck. Bandages wrapped tight around his thigh beneath torn dark-washed jeans, and Victor's knuckles were warm and familiar under his palm, resting on the gear shifter.

"I still have that lemon you asked me to get," Michael said.

Victor smirked. "Cooking with lemon is known to strengthen relationships and show true intentions. It's for clarity. Healing too."

"And?"

"I was going to make you lemon cookies," he said matter-of-factly. He glanced at Michael, brow lifted, smile lopsided and true. "I still can if you want."

Michael's cheek heated, his heart skipped and stuttered, and he brought Victor's knuckles to his lips. "Yeah, I'd like that."

A green sign along the highway—*Now Leaving Port Lewis*—rushed by the window.

The ocean was on his right, waves crashing against tall cliffs, and Victor's fingers were laced with his. Music came through the speakers, melodic, bassy electronica. Elizabeth perched comfortably on the dashboard, all eight pink toes seated on an empty felt bag.

His past was behind him. Adventure was in front of him. Victor Lewellyn was beside him.

Michael smiled and turned up the music.

Impossible? No. Not a damn thing was impossible. Not this.

Not them.

# About the Author

Brooklyn Ray is a tea connoisseur and an occult junkie. She writes queer speculative fiction layered with magic, rituals, and found families.

Twitter: @brookieraywrite

Goodreads:
www.goodreads.com/author/show/16971356.Brooklyn_Ray

# Other books by this author

*Darkling*
*Undertow*

# Also Available from NineStar Press

# Connect with NineStar Press

www.ninestarpress.com

www.facebook.com/ninestarpress

www.facebook.com/groups/NineStarNiche

www.twitter.com/ninestarpress

www.tumblr.com/blog/ninestarpress

Made in the USA
Coppell, TX
26 May 2020